Towards

Towards the Goal

by Mrs. Humphry Ward

Copyright © 1/29/2016
Jefferson Publication

ISBN-13: 978-1523772865

Printed in the United States of America

Table of Contents

INTRODUCTION

England has in this war reached a height of achievement loftier than that which she attained in the struggle with Napoleon; and she has reached that height in a far shorter period. Her giant effort, crowned with a success as wonderful as the effort itself, is worthily described by the author of this book. Mrs. Ward writes nobly on a noble theme.

This war is the greatest the world has ever seen. The vast size of the armies, the tremendous slaughter, the loftiness of the heroism shown, and the hideous horror of the brutalities committed, the valour of the fighting men, and the extraordinary ingenuity of those who have designed and built the fighting machines, the burning patriotism of the people who defend their hearthstones, and the far-reaching complexity of the plans of the leaders—all are on a scale so huge that nothing in past history can be compared with them. The issues at stake are elemental. The free peoples of the world have banded together against tyrannous militarism and government by caste. It is not too much to say that the outcome will largely determine, for daring and liberty-loving souls, whether or not life is worth living. A Prussianised world would be as intolerable as a world ruled over by Attila or by Timur the Lame.

It is in this immense world-crisis that England has played her part; a part which has grown greater month by month. Mrs. Ward enables us to see the awakening of the national soul which rendered it possible to play this part; and she describes the works by which the faith of the soul justified itself.

What she writes is of peculiar interest to the United States. We have suffered, or are suffering, in exaggerated form, from most (not all) of the evils that were eating into the fibre of the British character three years ago—and in addition from some purely indigenous ills of our own. If we are to cure ourselves it must be by our own exertions; our destiny will certainly not be shaped for us, as was Germany's, by a few towering autocrats of genius, such as Bismarck and Moltke. Mrs. Ward shows us the people of England in the act of curing their own ills, of making good, by gigantic and self-sacrificing exertion in the present, the folly and selfishness and greed and soft slackness of the past. The fact that England, when on the brink of destruction, gathered her strength and strode resolutely back to safety, is a fact of happy omen for us in America, who are now just awaking to the folly and selfishness and greed and soft slackness that for some years we have been showing.

As in America, so in England, a surfeit of materialism had produced a lack of high spiritual purpose in the nation at large; there was much confusion of ideas and ideals; and also much triviality, which was especially offensive when it masqueraded under some high-sounding name. An unhealthy sentimentality—the antithesis of morality—has gone hand in hand with a peculiarly sordid and repulsive materialism. The result was a soil in which various noxious weeds flourished rankly; and of these the most noxious was professional pacificism. The professional pacificist has at times festered in the diseased tissue of almost every civilisation; but it is only within the last three-quarters of a century that he has been a serious menace to the peace of justice and righteousness. In consequence, decent citizens are only beginning to understand the base immorality of his preaching and practice; and he has been given entirely undeserved credit for good intentions. In England as in the United States, domestic pacificism has been the most potent ally of alien militarism. And in both countries the extreme type has shown itself profoundly unpatriotic. The damage it has done the nation has been limited only by its weakness and folly; those who have professed it have served the devil to the full extent which their limited powers permitted.

There were in England—just as there are now in America—even worse foes to national honour and efficiency. Greed and selfishness, among capitalists and among labour leaders, had to be grappled with. The sordid baseness which saw in the war only a chance for additional money profits to the employer was almost matched by the fierce selfishness which refused to consider a strike from any but the standpoint of the strikers.

But the chief obstacle to be encountered in rousing England was sheer short-sightedness. A considerable time elapsed before it was possible to make the people understand that this was a people's war, that it was a matter of vital personal concern to the people as a whole, and to all individuals as individuals. In America we are now encountering much the same difficulties, due to much the same causes.

In England the most essential thing to be done was to wake the people to their need, and to guide them in meeting the need. The next most essential was to show to them, and to the peoples in friendly lands, whether allied or neutral, how the task was done; and this both as a reason for just pride in what had been achieved and as an inspiration to further effort.

Mrs. Ward's books—her former book and her present one—accomplish both purposes. Every American who reads the present volume must feel a hearty and profound respect for the patriotism, energy, and efficiency shown by the British people when they became awake to the nature of the crisis; and furthermore, every American must feel stirred with the desire to see his country now emulate Britain's achievement.

In this volume Mrs. Ward draws a wonderful picture of the English in the full tide of their successful effort. From the beginning England's naval effort and her money effort have been extraordinary. By the time Mrs. Ward's first book was written, the work of industrial preparedness was in full blast; but it could yet not be said that England's army in the field was the equal of the huge, carefully prepared, thoroughly coordinated military machines of those against whom and beside whom it fought. Now, the English army is itself as fine and as highly efficient a military machine as the wisdom of man can devise; now, the valour and hardihood of the individual soldier are being utilised to the full under a vast and perfected system which enables those in control of the great engine to use every unit in such fashion as to aid in driving the mass forward to victory.

Even the Napoleonic contest was child's play compared to this. Never has Great Britain been put to such a test. Never since the spacious days of Elizabeth has she been in such danger. Never, in any crisis, has she risen to so lofty a height of self-sacrifice and achievement. In the giant struggle against Napoleon, England's own safety was secured by the demoralisation of the French fleet. But in this contest the German naval authorities have at their disposal a fleet of extraordinary efficiency, and have devised for use on an extended scale the most formidable and destructive of all instruments of marine warfare. In previous coalitions England has partially financed her continental allies; in this case the expenditures have been on an unheard-of scale, and in consequence England's industrial strength, in men and money, in business and mercantile and agricultural ability, has been drawn on as never before. As in the days of Marlborough and Wellington, so now, England has sent her troops to the continent; but whereas formerly her expeditionary forces, although of excellent quality, were numerically too small to be of primary importance, at present her army is already, by size as well as by excellence, a factor of prime importance, in the military situation; and its relative as well as absolute importance is steadily growing.

And to her report of the present stage of Great Britain's effort in the war, Mrs. Ward has added some letters describing from her own personal experience the ruin wrought by the Germans in towns like Senlis and Gerbéviller, and in the hundreds of villages in Northern, Central, and Eastern France that now lie wrecked and desolate. And she has told in detail, and from the evidence of eye-witnesses, some of the piteous incidents of German cruelty to the civilian population, which are already burnt into the conscience of Europe, and should never be forgotten till reparation has been made.

Mrs. Ward's book is thus of high value as a study of contemporary history. It is of at least as high value as an inspiration to constructive patriotism.

THEODORE ROOSEVELT.

SAGAMORE HILLS,

May 1st, 1917.

TOWARDS THE GOAL

No. 1

March 24th, 1917.

DEAR MR. ROOSEVELT,—It may be now frankly confessed—(you, some time ago, gave me leave to publish your original letter, as it might seem opportune)—that it was you who gave the impulse last year, which led to the writing of the first series of Letters on "England's Effort" in the war, which were published in book form in June 1916. Your appeal—that I should write a general account for America of the part played by England in the vast struggle—found me in our quiet country house, busy with quite other work, and at first I thought it impossible that I could attempt so new a task as you proposed to me. But support and encouragement came from our own authorities, and like many other thousands of English women under orders, I could only go and do my best. I spent some time in the Munition areas, watching the enormous and rapid development of our war industries and of the astonishing part played in it by women; I was allowed to visit a portion of the Fleet, and finally, to spend twelve days in France, ten of them among the great supply bases and hospital camps, with two days at the British Headquarters, and on the front, near Poperinghe, and Richebourg St. Vaast.

The result was a short book which has been translated into many foreign tongues—French, Italian, Dutch, German, Russian, Portuguese, and Japanese—which has brought me many American letters from many different States, and has been perhaps most widely read of all among our own people. For we all read newspapers, and we all forget them! In this vast and changing struggle, events huddle on each other, so that the new blurs and wipes out the old. There is always room—is there not?—for such a personal narrative as may recall to us the main outlines, and the chief determining factors of a war in which—often—everything seems to us in flux, and our eyes, amid the tumult of the stream, are apt to lose sight of the landmarks on its bank, and the signs of the approaching goal.

And now again—after a year—I have been attempting a similar task, with renewed and cordial help from our authorities at home and abroad. And I venture to address these new Letters directly to yourself, as to that American of all others to whom this second chapter on England's Effort may look for sympathy. Whither are we tending—your country and mine? Congress meets on April 1st. Before this Letter reaches you great decisions will have been taken. I will not attempt to speculate. The logic of facts will sweep our nations together in some sort of intimate union—of that I have no doubt.

How much further, then, has Great Britain marched since the Spring of last year—how much nearer is she to the end? One can but answer such questions in the most fragmentary and tentative way, relying for the most part on the opinions and information of those who know, those who are in the van of action, at home and abroad, but also on one's own personal impressions of an incomparable scene. And every day, almost, at this breathless moment, the answer of yesterday may become obsolete.

I left our Headquarters in France, for instance, some days before the news of the Russian revolution reached London, and while the Somme retirement was still in its earlier stages. Immediately afterwards the events of one short week transformed the whole political aspect of Europe, and may well prove to have changed the face of the war—although as to that, let there be no dogmatising yet! But before the pace becomes faster still, and before the unfolding of those great and perhaps final events we may now dimly foresee, let me try and seize the impressions of some memorable weeks and bring them to bear—so far as the war is concerned—on those questions which, in the present state of affairs, must interest you in America scarcely less than they interest us here. Where, in fact, do we stand?

Any kind of answer must begin with the Navy. For, in the case of Great Britain, and indeed scarcely less in the case of the Allies, that is the foundation of everything. To yourself the facts will all be familiar—but for the benefit of those innumerable friends of the Allies in Europe and America whom I would fain reach with the help of your great name, I will run through a few of the recent—the ground—facts of the past year, as I myself ran through them a few days ago, before, with an Admiralty permit, I went down to one of the most interesting naval bases on our coast and found myself amid a group of men engaged night and day in grappling with the submarine menace which threatens not only Great Britain, not only the Allies, but yourselves, and every neutral nation. It is well to go back to these facts. They are indeed worthy of this island nation, and her seaborn children.

To begin with, the *personnel* of the British Navy, which at the beginning of the war was 140,000, was last year 300,000. This year it is 400,000, or very nearly three times what it was before the war. Then as to ships,—"If we were strong in capital ships at the beginning of the war"—said Mr. Balfour, last September, "we are yet stronger now—absolutely and relatively—and in regard to cruisers and destroyers there is absolutely no comparison between our strength in 1914 and our strength now. There is no part of our naval strength in which we have not got a greater supply, and in some departments an incomparably greater supply than we had on August 4th, 1914.... The tonnage of the Navy has increased by well over a million tons since war began."

So Mr. Balfour, six months ago. Five months later, it fell to Sir Edward Carson to move the naval estimates, under pressure, as we all know, of the submarine anxiety. He spoke in the frankest and plainest language of that anxiety, as did the Prime Minister in his now famous speech of February 22nd, and as did the speakers in the House of Lords, Lord Lytton, Lord Curzon and Lord Beresford, on the same date. *The attack is not yet checked. The danger is not over.* Still again—look at some of the facts! In two years and a quarter of war—

Eight million men moved across the seas—almost without mishap.

Nine million and a half tons of explosives carried to our own armies and those of our Allies.

Over a million horses and mules; and—

Over forty-seven million gallons of petrol supplied to the armies.

And besides, twenty-five thousand ships have been examined for contraband of war, on the high seas, or in harbour, since the war began.

And at this, one must pause a moment to think—once again—what it means; to call up the familiar image of Britain's ships, large and small, scattered over the wide Atlantic and the approaches to the North Sea, watching there through winter and summer, storm and fair, and so carrying out, relentlessly, the blockade of Germany, through every circumstance often of danger and difficulty; with every consideration for neutral interests that is compatible with this desperate war, in which the very existence of England is concerned; and without the sacrifice of a single life, unless it be the lives of British sailors, often lost in these boardings of passing ships, amid the darkness and storm of winter seas. There, indeed, in these "wave-beaten" ships, as in the watching fleets of the English Admirals outside Toulon and Brest, while Napoleon was marching triumphantly about Europe, lies the root fact of the war. It is a commonplace, but one that has been "proved upon our pulses." Who does not remember the shock that went through England—and the civilised world—when the first partial news of the Battle of Jutland reached London, and we were told our own losses, before we knew either the losses of the enemy or the general result of the battle? It was neither fear, nor panic; but it was as though the nation, holding its breath, realised for the first time where, for it, lay the vital elements of being. The depths in us were stirred. We knew in very deed that we were the children of the sea!

And now again the depths are stirred. The development of the submarine attack has set us a new and stern task, and we are "straitened till it be accomplished." The great battle-ships seem almost to have left the stage. In less than three months, 626,000 tons of British, neutral and allied shipping have been destroyed. Since the beginning of the war we—Great Britain—have lost over two million tons of shipping, and our Allies and the neutrals have lost almost as much. There is a certain shortage of food in Great Britain, and a shortage of many other things besides. Writing about the middle of February, an important German newspaper raised a shout of jubilation. "The whole sea was as if swept clean at one blow"—by the announcement of the intensified "blockade" of the first of February. So the German scribe. But again the facts shoot up, hard and irreducible, through the sea of comment. While the German newspapers were shouting to each other, the sea was so far from being "swept clean," that twelve thousand ships had actually passed in and out of British ports in the first eighteen days of the "blockade." And at any moment during those days, at least 3,000 ships could have been found traversing the "danger zone," which the Germans imagined themselves to have barred. One is reminded of the *Hamburger Nachrichten* last year, after the Zeppelin raid in January 1916. "English industry lies in ruins," said that astonishing print. "The sea has been swept clean," says one of its brethren now. Yet all the while, there, in the danger zone, whenever, by day or night, one turns one's thoughts to it, are the three thousand ships; and there in the course of a fortnight, are the twelve thousand ships going and coming.

Yet all the same, as I have said before, there is danger and there is anxiety. The neutrals—save America—have been intimidated; they are keeping their ships in harbour; and to do without their tonnage is a serious matter for us. Meanwhile, the best brains in naval England are at work, and one can feel the sailors straining at the leash. In the first eighteen days of February, there were forty fights with submarines. The Navy talks very little about them, and says nothing of which it is not certain. But all the scientific resources, all the fighting brains of naval England are being brought to bear, and we at home—well, let us keep to our rations, the only thing we can do to help our men at sea!

How this grey estuary spread before my eyes illustrates and illuminates the figures I have been quoting! I am on the light cruiser of a famous Commodore, and I have just been creeping and climbing through a submarine. The waters round are crowded with those light craft, destroyers, submarines, mine-sweepers, trawlers, patrol boats, on which for the moment at any rate the fortunes of the naval war turns. And take notice that they are all—or almost all—*new*; the very latest products of British ship-yards. We have plenty of battle-ships, but "we must now build, as quickly as possible, the smaller craft, and the merchant ships we want," says Sir Edward Carson. "Not a slip in the country will be empty during the coming months. Every rivet put into a ship will contribute to the defeat of Germany. And 47 per cent, of the Merchant Service have already been armed." The riveters must indeed have been hard at work! This crowded scene carries me back to the Clyde where I was last year, to the new factories and workshops, with their ever-increasing throng of women, and to the marvellous work of the ship-yards. No talk now of strikes, of a disaffected and revolutionary minority, on the Clyde, at any rate, as there was twelve months ago. Broadly speaking, and allowing for a small, stubborn, but insignificant Pacifist section, the will of the nation, throughout all classes, has become as steel—to win the war.

Throughout England, as in these naval officers beside me, there is the same tense yet disciplined expectancy. As we lunch and talk, on this cruiser at rest, messages come in perpetually; the cruiser itself is ready for the open sea, at an hour and a half's notice; the seaplanes pass out and come in over the mouth of the harbour on their voyages of discovery and report, and these destroyers and mine-sweepers that he so quietly near us will be out again to-night in the North Sea, grappling with every difficulty and facing every danger, in the true spirit of a wonderful service, while we land-folk sleep and eat in peace;—grumbling no doubt, with our morning newspaper and coffee, when any of the German destroyers who come out from Zeebrugge are allowed to get home with a whole skin. "What on earth is the Navy about?" Well, the Navy knows. Germany is doing her very worst, and will go on doing it—for a time. The line of defensive watch in the North Sea is long; the North Sea is a big place; the Germans often have the luck of the street-boy who rings a bell and runs away, before the policeman comes up. But the Navy has no doubts. The situation, says one of my cheerful hosts, is "quite healthy" and we shall see "great things in the coming months." We had better leave it at that!

Now let us look at these destroyers in another scene. It is the last day of February, and I find myself on a military steamer, bound for a French Port, and on my way to the British Headquarters in France. With me is the same dear daughter who accompanied me last year as "dame secrétaire" on my first errand. The boat is crowded with soldiers, and before we reach the French shore we have listened to almost every song—old and new—in Tommy's repertory. There

9

is even "Tipperary," a snatch, a ghost of "Tipperary," intermingled with many others, rising and falling, no one knows why, started now here, now there, and dying away again after a line or two. It is a draft going out to France for the first time, north countrymen, by their accent; and life-belts and submarines seem to amuse them hugely, to judge by the running fire of chaff that goes on. But, after a while, I cease to listen. I am thinking first of what awaits us on the further shore, on which the lights are coming out, and of those interesting passes inviting us to G.H.Q. as "Government Guests," which lie safe in our handbags. And then, my thoughts slip back to a conversation of the day before, with Dr. Addison, the new Minister of Munitions.

A man in the prime of life, with whitening hair—prematurely white, for the face and figure are quite young still—and stamped, so far as expression and aspect are concerned, by those social and humane interests which first carried him into Parliament. I have been long concerned with Evening Play Centres for school-children in Hoxton, one of the most congested quarters of our East End. And seven years ago I began to hear of the young and public-spirited doctor and man of science, who had made himself a name and place in Hoxton, who had won the confidence of the people crowded in its unlovely streets, had worked for the poor, and the sick, and the children, and had now beaten the Tory member, and was Hoxton's Liberal representative in the new Parliament elected in January 1910, to deal with the Lords, after the throwing out of Lloyd George's famous Budget. Once or twice since, I had come across him in matters concerned with education—cripple schools and the like—when he was Parliamentary Secretary to the Board of Education, immediately before the war. And now here was the doctor, the Hunterian Professor, the social worker, the friend of schools and school-children, transformed into the fighting Minister of a great fighting Department, itself the creation of the war, only second—if second—in its importance for the war, to the Admiralty and the War Office.

I was myself, for a fortnight of last year, the guest of the Ministry of Munitions, while Mr. Lloyd George was still its head, in some of the most important Munition areas; and I was then able to feel the current of hot energy, started by the first Minister, running—not of course without local obstacles and animosities—through an electrified England. That was in February 1916. Then, in August, came the astonishing speech of Mr. Montagu, on the development of the Munitions supply in one short year, as illustrated by the happenings of the Somme battlefield. And now, as successor to Mr. Montagu and Mr. Lloyd George, Dr. Addison sat in the Minister's chair, continuing the story.

What a story it is! Starting from the manufacture of guns, ammunition and explosives, and after pushing that to incredible figures, the necessities of its great task has led the Ministry to one forward step after another. Seeing that the supply of munitions depends on the supply of raw material, it is now regulating the whole mineral supply of this country, and much of that of the Allies; it is about to work qualities of iron ore that have never been worked before; it is deciding, over the length and breadth of the country, how much aluminium should be allowed to one firm, how much copper to another; it is producing steel for our Allies as well as for ourselves; it has taken over with time the whole

Motor Transport of the war, and is now adding to it the Railway Transport of munitions here and abroad, and is dictating meanwhile to every engineering firm in the country which of its orders should come first, and which last. It is managing a whole gigantic industry with employes running into millions, half a million of them women, and managing it under wholly new conditions of humanity and forethought; it is housing and feeding and caring for innumerable thousands; transforming from day to day, as by a kind of by-work, the industrial mind and training of multitudes, and laying the foundations of a new, and surely happier England, after the War. And, finally, it is adjusting, with, on the whole, great success, the rival claims of the factories and the trenches, sending more and more men from the workshops to the fighting line, in proportion as the unskilled labour of the country—men and women, but especially women—is drawn, more and more widely, into the service of a dwindling amount of skilled labour, more and more "diluted."

* * * * *

But the light is failing and the shore is nearing. Life-belts are taken off, the destroyers have disappeared. We are on the quay, kindly welcomed by an officer from G.H.Q. who passes our bags rapidly through the Custom House, and carries us off to a neighbouring hotel for the night, it being too late for the long drive to G.H.Q. We are in France again!—and the great presence of the army is all about us. The quay crowded with soldiers, the port alive with ships, the grey-blue uniforms mingling with the khaki—after a year I see it again, and one's pulses quicken. The vast "effort of England" which last year had already reached so great a height, and has now, as all accounts testify, been so incredibly developed, is here once more in visible action, before me.

Next day, the motor arrives early, and with our courteous officer who has charge of us, in front, we are off, first, for one of the great camps I saw last year, and then for G.H.Q. itself. On the way, as we speed over the rolling down country beyond the town, my eyes are keen to catch some of the new signs of the time. Here is the first—a railway line in process of doubling—and large numbers of men, some of them German prisoners, working at it; typical both of the immense railway development all over the military zone, since last year, and of the extensive use now being made of prisoners' labour, in regions well behind the firing line. They lift their heads, as we pass, looking with curiosity at the two ladies in the military car. Their flat round caps give them an odd similarity. It is as if one saw scores of the same face, differentiated here and there by a beard. A docile hard-working crew, by all accounts, who give no trouble, and are managed largely by their N.C.O.'s. Are there some among them who saw the massacre at Dinant, the terrible things in Lorraine? Their placid, expressionless faces tell no tale.

But the miles have flown, and here already are the long lines of the camp. How pleasant to be greeted by some of the same officers! We go into the Headquarters Office, for a talk. "Grown? I should think we have!" says Colonel——. And, rapidly, he and one of his colleagues run through some of the additions and expansions. The Training Camp has been practically doubled, or, rather, another training camp has been added to the one that existed last year,

11

and both are equipped with an increased number of special schools—an Artillery Training School, an Engineer Training School, a Lewis Gun School, a Gas School, with an actual gas chamber for the training of men in the use of their gas helmets,—and others, of which it is not possible to speak. "We have put through half a million of reinforcements since you were here last." And close upon two million rations were issued last month! The veterinary accommodation has been much enlarged, and two Convalescent Horse Depots have been added—(it is good indeed to see with what kindness and thought the Army treats its horses!). But the most novel addition to the camp has been a Fat Factory for the production of fat,—from which comes the glycerine used in explosives—out of all the food refuse of the camp. The fat produced by the system, here and in England, has already provided glycerine *far millions of eighteen-pounder shells*; the problem of camp refuse, always a desperate one, has been solved; and as a commercial venture the factory makes 250 per cent. profit.

Undeterred by what we hear of the smells! we go off to see it, and the enthusiastic manager explains the unsavoury processes by which the bones and refuse of all the vast camp are boiled down into a white fat, that looks *almost* eatable, but is meant, as a matter of fact, to feed not men but shells. Nor is that the only contribution to the fighting line which the factory makes. All the cotton waste of the hospitals, with their twenty thousand beds—the old dressings and bandages—come here, and after sterilisation and disinfection go to England for gun-cotton. Was there ever a grimmer cycle than this, by which that which feeds, and that which heals, becomes in the end that which kills! But let me try to forget that side of it, and remember, rather, as we leave the smells behind, that the calcined bones become artificial manure, and go back again into the tortured fields of France, while other bye-products of the factory help the peasants near to feed their pigs. And anything, however small, that helps the peasants of France in this war, comforts one's heart.

We climb up to the high ground of the camp for a general view before we go on to G.H.Q. and I see it, as I saw it last year, spread under the March sunshine, among the sand and the pines—a wonderful sight. "Everything has grown, you see, except the staff!" says the Colonel, smiling, as we shake hands. "But we rub along!"

Then we are in the motor again, and at last the new G.H.Q.—how different from that I saw last year!—rises before us. We make our way into the town, and presently the car stops for a minute before a building, and while our officer goes within, we retreat into a side street to wait. But my thoughts are busy. For that building, of which the side-front is still visible, is the brain of the British Army in France, and on the men who work there depend the fortunes of that distant line where our brothers and sons are meeting face to face the horrors and foulnesses of war. How many women whose hearts hang on the war, whose all is there, in daily and nightly jeopardy, read the words "British Headquarters" with an involuntary lift of soul, an invocation without words! Yet scarcely half a dozen Englishwomen in this war will ever see the actual spot. And here it is, under my eyes, the cold March sun shining fitfully on it, the sentry at the door, the khaki figures passing in and out. I picture to myself the rooms within, and the news arriving of General Gough's advance on the Ancre, of that German retreat as to which all Europe is speculating.

But we move on—to a quiet country house in a town garden—the Headquarters Mess of the Intelligence Department. Here I find, among our kind hosts, men already known to me from my visit of the year before, men whose primary business it is to watch the enemy, who know where every German regiment and German Commander are, who through the aerial photography of our airmen are now acquainted with every step of the German retreat, and have already the photographs of his second line. All the information gathered from prisoners, and from innumerable other sources, comes here; and the department has its eye besides on everything that happens within the zone of our Armies in France. For a woman to be received here is an exception—perhaps I may say an honour—of which I am rather tremulously aware. Can I make it worth while? But a little conversation with these earnest and able men shows plainly that they have considered the matter like any other incident in the day's work. *England's Effort* has been useful; therefore I am to be allowed again to see and write for myself; and therefore, what information can be given me as to the growth of our military power in France since last year will be given. It is not, of course, a question of war correspondence, which is not within a woman's powers. But it is a question of as much "seeing" as can be arranged for, combined with as much first-hand information as time and the censor allow. I begin to see my way.

The conversation at luncheon—the simplest of meals—and during a stroll afterwards, is thrilling indeed to us newcomers. "The coming summer's campaign *must* decide the issue of the war—though it may not see the end of it." "The issue of the war"—and the fate of Europe! "An inconclusive peace would be a victory for Germany." There is no doubt here as to the final issue; but there is a resolute refusal to fix dates, or prophesy details. "Man for man we are now the better army. Our strength is increasing month by month, while that of Germany is failing. Men and officers, who a year ago were still insufficiently trained, are now seasoned troops with nothing to learn from the Germans; and the troops recruited under the Military Service Act, now beginning to come out, are of surprisingly good quality." On such lines the talk runs, and it is over all too soon.

Then we are in the motor again, bound for an aerodrome forty or fifty miles away. We are late, and the last twenty-seven kilometres fly by in thirty-two minutes! It is a rolling country, and there are steep descents and sharp climbs, through the thickly-scattered and characteristic villages and small old towns of the Nord, villages crowded all of them with our men. Presently, with a start, we find ourselves on a road which saw us last spring—a year ago, to the day. The same blue distances, the same glimpses of old towns in the hollows, the same touches of snow on the heights. At last, in the cold sunset light, we draw up at our destination. The wide aerodrome stretches before us—great hangars coloured so as to escape the notice of a Boche overhead—with machines of all sizes, rising and landing—coming out of the hangars, or returning to them for the night. Two of the officers in charge meet us, and I walk round with them, looking at the various types—some for fighting, some for observation; and

13

understanding—what I can! But the spirit of the men—that one can understand. "We are accumulating, concentrating now, for the summer offensive. Of course the Germans have been working hard too. They have lots of new and improved machines. But when the test comes we are confident that we shall down them again, as we did on the Somme. For us, the all-important thing is the fighting behind the enemy lines. Our object is to prevent the German machines from rising at all, to keep them down, while our airmen are reconnoitering along the fighting line. Awfully dangerous work! Lots don't come back. But what then? They will have done their job!"

The words were spoken so carelessly that for a few seconds I did not realise their meaning. But there was that in the expression of the man who spoke them which showed there was no lack of realisation there. How often I have recalled them, with a sore heart, in these recent weeks of heavy losses in the air-service—losses due, I have no doubt, to the special claims upon it of the German retreat.

The conversation dropped a little, till one of my companions, with a smile, pointed overhead. Three splendid biplanes were sailing above us, at a great height, bound south-wards. "Back from the line!" said the officer beside me, and we watched them till they dipped and disappeared in the sunset clouds. Then tea and pleasant talk. The young men insist that D. shall make tea. This visit of two ladies is a unique event. For the moment, as she makes tea in their sitting-room, which is now full of men, there is an illusion of home.

Then we are off, for another fifty miles. Darkness comes on, the roads are unfamiliar. At last an avenue and bright lights. We have reached the Visitors' Château, under the wing of G.H.Q.

No. 2

March 31st, 1917.

DEAR MR. ROOSEVELT,—My first letter you will perhaps remember took us to the Visitors' Château of G.H.Q. and left us alighting there, to be greeted by the same courteous host, Captain——, who presided last year over another Guest House far away. But we were not to sleep at the Château, which was already full of guests. Arrangements had been made for us at a cottage in the village near, belonging to the village schoolmistress; the motor took us there immediately, and after changing our travel-stained dresses, we went back to the Château for dinner. Many guests—all of them of course of the male sex, and much talk! Some of the guests—members of Parliament, and foreign correspondents—had been over the Somme battlefield that day, and gave alarmist accounts of the effects of the thaw upon the roads and the ground generally. Banished for a time by the frost, the mud had returned; and mud, on the front, becomes a kind of malignant force which affects the spirits of the soldiers.

The schoolmistress and her little maid sat up for us, and shepherded us kindly to bed. Never was there a more strangely built little house! The ceilings came down on our heads, the stairs were perpendicular. But there was a stove in each room, and the beds though hard, and the floor though bare, were scrupulously

14

clean. In the early morning I woke up and looked out. There had been a white frost, and the sun was just rising in a clear sky. Its yellow light was shining on the whitewashed wall of the next cottage, on which a large pear-tree was trained. All round were frost-whitened plots of garden or meadow—*préaux*—with tall poplars in the hedges cutting the morning sky. Suddenly, I heard a continuous murmur in the room beneath me. It was the schoolmistress and her maid at prayer. And presently the house door opened and shut. It was Mademoiselle who had gone to early Mass. For the school was an *école libre*, and the little lady who taught it was a devout Catholic. The rich yet cold light, the frosty quiet of the village, the thin French trees against the sky, the ritual murmur in the room below—it was like a scene from a novel by René Bazin, and breathed the old, the traditional France.

We were to start early and motor far, but there was time before we started for a little talk with Mademoiselle. She was full of praise for our English soldiers, some of whom were billeted in the village. "They are very kind to our people, they often help the women, and they never complain." (Has the British Tommy in these parts really forgotten how to grouse?) "I had some of your men billeted here. I could only give them a room without beds, just the bare boards. 'You will find it hard,' I said. 'We will get a little straw,' said the sergeant. 'That will be all right.' Our men would have grumbled." (But I think this was Mademoiselle's *politesse*!) "And the children are devoted to your soldiers. I have a dear little girl in the school, nine years old. Sometimes from the window she sees a man in the street, a soldier who lodges with her mother. Then I cannot hold her. She is like a wild thing to be gone. 'Voilà mon camarade!—voilà mon camarade!' Out she goes, and is soon walking gravely beside him, hand in hand, looking up at him." "How do they understand each other?" "I don't know. But they have a language. Your sergeants often know more French than your officers, because they have to do the billeting and the talking to our people."

The morning was still bright when the motor arrived, but the frost had been keen, and the air on the uplands was biting. We speed first across a famous battlefield, where French and English bones lie mingled below the quiet grass, and then turn south-east. Nobody on the roads. The lines of poplar-trees fly past, the magpies flutter from the woods, and one might almost forget the war. Suddenly, a railway line, a steep descent and we are full in its midst again. On our left an encampment of Nissen huts—so called from their inventor, a Canadian officer—those new and ingenious devices for housing troops, or labour battalions, or coloured workers, at an astonishing saving both of time and material. In shape like the old-fashioned beehive, each hut can be put up by four or six men in a few hours. Everything is, of course, standardised, and the wood which lines their corrugated iron is put together in the simplest and quickest ways, ways easily suggested, no doubt, to the Canadian mind, familiar with "shacks" and lumber camps. We shall come across them everywhere along the front. But on this first occasion my attention is soon distracted from them, for as we turn a corner beyond the hut settlement, which I am told is that of a machine-gun detachment, there is an exclamation from D——.

15

Tanks! The officer in front points smiling to a field just ahead. There is one of them—the monster!—taking its morning exercise; practising up and down the high and almost perpendicular banks by which another huge field is divided. The motor slackens, and we watch the creature slowly attack a high bank, land complacently on the top, and then—an officer walking beside it to direct its movements—balance a moment on the edge of another bank equally high, a short distance away. There it is!—down!—not flopping or falling, but all in the way of business, gliding unperturbed. London is full of tanks, of course—on the films. But somehow to be watching a real one, under the French sky, not twenty miles from the line, is a different thing. We fall into an eager discussion with Captain F. in front, as to the part played by them in the Somme battle, and as to what the Germans may be preparing in reply to them. And while we talk, my eye is caught by something on the sky-line, just above the tank. It is a man and a plough—a plough that might have come out of the Odyssey—the oldest, simplest type. So are the ages interwoven; and one may safely guess that the plough—that very type!—will outlast many generations of tanks. But, for the moment, the tanks are in the limelight, and it is luck that we should have come upon them so soon, for one may motor many miles about the front without meeting with any signs of them.

Next, a fine main road and an old town, seething with all the stir of war. We come upon a crowded market-place, and two huge convoys passing each other in the narrow street beyond—one, an ammunition column, into which our motor humbly fits itself as best it can, by order of the officer in charge of the column, and the other, a long string of magnificent lorries belonging to the Flying Corps, which defiles past us on the left. The inhabitants of the town, old men, women and children, stand to watch the hubbub, with amused friendly faces. On we go, for a time, in the middle of the convoy. The great motor lorries filled with ammunition hem us in till the town is through, and a long hill is climbed. At the top of it we are allowed to draw out, and motor slowly past long lines of troops on the march; first, R.E.'s with their store waggons, large and small; then a cyclist detachment; a machine-gun detachment; field kitchens, a white goat lying lazily on the top of one of them; mules, heavily laden; and Lewis guns in little carts. Then infantry marching briskly in the keen air, while along other roads, visible to east and west, we see other columns converging. A division, apparently, on the march. The physique of the men, their alert and cheerful looks, strike me particularly. This pitiless war seems to have revealed to England herself the quality of her race. Though some credit must be given to the physical instructors of the Army!—who in the last twelve months especially have done a wonderful work.

At last we turn out of the main road, and the endless columns pass away into the distance. Again, a railway line in process of doubling; beyond, a village, which seems to be mainly occupied by an Army Medical detachment; then two large Casualty Clearing Stations, and a Divisional Dressing Station. Not many wounded here at present; the section of the line from which we are only some ten miles distant has been comparatively quiet of late. But what preparations everywhere! What signs of the coming storm! Hardly a minute passes as we speed along without its significant sight; horse-lines, Army Service depots bursting with stores,—a great dump of sandbags—another of ammunition.

And as I look out at the piles of shells, I think of the most recent figures furnished me by the Ministry of Munitions. Last year, when the Somme offensive began, and when I was writing *England's Effort*, the *weekly* output of eighteen-pounder shells was 17-1/2 times what it was during the first year of the war. *It is now* 28 *times as much.* Field howitzer ammunition has *almost doubled* since last July. That of medium guns and howitzers *has more than doubled.* That of the heaviest guns of all (over six-inch) *is more than four times* as great. By the growth of ammunition we may guess what has been the increase in guns, especially in those heavy guns we are now pushing forward after the retreating Germans, as fast as roads and railway lines can be made to carry them. The German Government, through one of its subordinate spokesmen, has lately admitted their inferiority in guns; their retreat, indeed, on the Somme before our pending attack, together with the state of their old lines, now we are in and over them, show plainly enough what they had to fear from the British guns and the abundance of British ammunition.

But what are these strange figures swarming beside the road—black tousled heads and bronze faces? Kaffir "boys," at work in some quarries, feeling the cold, no doubt, on this bright bitter day, in spite of their long coats. They are part of that large body of native labour, Chinese, Kaffir, Basuto, which is now helping our own men everywhere to push on and push up, as the new labour forces behind them release more and more of the fighting men for that dogged pursuit which is going on *there*—in that blue distance to our right!—where the German line swings stubbornly back, south-east, from the Vimy Ridge.

The motor stops. This is a Headquarters, and a staff officer comes out to greet us—a boy in looks, but a D.S.O. all the same! His small car precedes us as a guide, and we keep up with him as best we may. These are mining villages we are passing through, and on the horizon are some of those pyramidal slag-heaps—the Fosses—which have seen some of the fiercest fighting of the war. But we leave the villages behind, and are soon climbing into a wooden upland. Suddenly, a halt. A notice-board forbids the use of a stretch of road before us "from sun-rise to sunset." Evidently it is under German observation. We try to find another, parallel. But here, too, the same notice confronts us. We dash along it, however, and my pulses run a little quicker, as I realise, from the maps we carry, how near we are to the enemy lines which lie hidden in the haze, eastward; and from my own eyes, how exposed is the hillside. But we are safely through, and a little further we come to a wood—a charming wood, to all seeming, of small trees, which in a week or two will be full of spring leaf and flower. But we are no sooner in it, jolting up its main track, than we understand the grimness of what it holds. Spring and flowers have not much to say to it! For this wood and its neighbourhood—Ablain St. Nazaire, Carency, Neuville St. Vaast—have seen war at its cruellest; thousands of brave lives have been yielded here; some of the dead are still lying unburied in its furthest thickets, and men will go softly through it in the years to come. "Stranger, go and tell the Lacedaemonians that we lie here, obedient to their will:"—the immortal words are in my ears. But how many are the sacred spots in this land for which they speak!

We leave the motor and walk on through the wood to the bare upland beyond. The wood is still a wood of death, actual or potential. Our own batteries are all about us; so too are the remains of French batteries, from the days when the French still held this portion of the line. We watch the gunners among the trees and presently pass an encampment of their huts. Beyond, a high and grassy plateau—fringes of wood on either hand. But we must not go to the edge on our right so as to look down into the valley below. Through the thin leafless trees, however, we see plainly the ridges that stretch eastward, one behind the other, "suffused in sunny air." There are the towers of Mont St. Eloy—ours; the Bertonval Wood—ours; and the famous Vimy Ridge, blue in the middle distance, of which half is ours and half German. We are very near the line. Notre Dame de Lorette is not very far away, though too far for us to reach the actual spot, the famous bluff, round which the battle raged in 1915. And now the guns begin!—the first we have heard since we arrived. From our left—as it seemed— some distance away, came the short sharp reports of the trench mortars, but presently, as we walked on, guns just behind us and below us, began to boom over our heads, and we heard again the long-drawn scream or swish of the shells, rushing on their deadly path to search out the back of the enemy's lines in the haze yonder, and flinging confusion on his lines of communication, his supplies and reserves. He does not reply. He has indeed been strangely meek of late. The reason here cannot be that he is slipping away from our attack, as is the case farther south. The Vimy Ridge is firmly held; it is indeed the pivot of the retreat. Perhaps to-day he is economising. But, of course, at any moment he might reply. After a certain amount of hammering he *must* reply! And there are some quite fresh shell-holes along our path, some of them not many hours old. Altogether, it is with relief that as the firing grows hotter we turn back and pick up the motor in the wood again.

And yet one is loath to go! Never again shall I stand in such a scene—never again behold those haunted ridges, and this wood of death with the guns that hide in it! To have shared ever so little in such a bit of human experience is for a woman a thing of awe, if one has time to think of it. Not even groups of artillery men, chatting or completing their morning's toilet, amid the thin trees, can dull that sense in me. *They* are only "strafing" Fritz or making ready to "strafe" him; they have had an excellent midday meal in the huts yonder, and they whistle and sing as they go about their work, disappearing sometimes into mysterious regions out of sight. That is all there is in it for them. They are "doing their job," like the airmen, and if a German shell finds them in the wood, why, the German will have done *his* job, and they will bear no grudge. It is simple as that—for them. But to the onlooker, they are all figures in a great design—woven into the terrible tapestry of war, and charged with a meaning that we of this actual generation shall never more than dimly see or understand.

Again we rush along the exposed road and back into the mining region, taking a westward turn. A stately chateau, and near it a smaller house, where a General greets us. Lunch is over, for we are late, but it is hospitably brought back for us, and the General and I plunge into talk of the retreat, of what it means for the Germans, and what it will mean for us. After luncheon, we go into the next room to look at the General's big maps which show clearly how the salients run, the smaller and the larger, from which the Germans are falling back, followed closely by the troops of General Gough. News of the condition of the enemy's abandoned lines is coming in fast. "Let no one make any mistake. They have gone because they *must*—because of the power of our artillery, which never stops hammering them, whether on the line or behind the line, which interferes with all their communications and supplies, and makes life intolerable. At the same time, the retreat is being skilfully done, and will of course delay us. That was why they did it. We shall have to push up roads, railways, supplies; the bringing up of the heavy guns will take time, but less time than they think! Our men are in the pink of condition!"

On which again follows very high praise of the quality of the men now coming out under the Military Service Act. "Yet they are conscripts," says one of us, in some surprise, "and the rest were volunteers." "No doubt. But these are the men—many of them—who had to balance duties—who had wives and children to leave, and businesses which depended on them personally. Compulsion has cut the knot and eased their consciences. They'll make fine soldiers! But we want more—*more!*" And then follows talk on the wonderful developments of training—even since last year; and some amusing reminiscences of the early days of England's astounding effort, by which vast mobs of eager recruits without guns, uniforms, or teachers, have been turned into the magnificent armies now fighting in France.

The War Office has lately issued privately some extremely interesting notes on the growth and training of the New Armies, of which it is only now possible to make public use. From these it is clear that in the Great Experiment of the first two years of war all phases of intellect and capacity have played their part. The widely trained mind, taking large views as to the responsibility of the Army towards the nation delivered into its hands, so that not only should it be disciplined for war but made fitter for peace; and the practical inventive gifts of individuals who, in seeking to meet a special need, stumble on something universal, both forces have been constantly at work. Discipline and initiative have been the twin conquerors, and the ablest men in the Army, to use a homely phrase, have been out for both. Many a fresh, and valuable bit of training has been due to some individual officer struck with a new idea, and patiently working it out. The special "schools," which are now daily increasing the efficiency of the Army, if you ask how they arose, you will generally be able to trace them back to some eager young man starting a modest experiment in his spare time for the teaching of himself and some of his friends, and so developing it that the thing is finally recognised, enlarged, and made the parent of similar efforts elsewhere.

Let me describe one such "school"—to me a thrilling one, as I saw it on a clear March afternoon. A year ago no such thing existed. Now each of our Armies possesses one.

But this letter is already too long!

No. 3

Easter Eve, 1917.

DEAR MR. ROOSEVELT,—Since I finished my last letter to you, before the meeting of Congress, great days have come and gone.

America is with us!

At last, we English folk can say that to each other, without reserve or qualification, and into England's mood of ceaseless effort and anxiety there has come a sudden relaxation, a breath of something canning and sustaining. What your action may be—whether it will shorten the war, and how much, no one here yet knows. But when in some great strain a friend steps to your side, you don't begin with questions. He is there. Your cause, your effort, are his. Details will come. Discussion will come. But there is a breathing space first, in which feeling rests upon itself before it rushes out in action. Such a breathing space for England are these Easter days!

Meanwhile, the letters from the Front come in with their new note of joy. "You should see the American faces in the Army to-day!" writes one. "They bring a new light into this dismal spring." How many of them? Mayn't we now confess to ourselves and our Allies that there is already, the equivalent of an American division, fighting with the Allied Armies in France, who have used every honest device to get there? They have come in by every channel, and under every pretext—wavelets, forerunners of the tide. For now, you too have to improvise great armies, as we improvised ours in the first two years of war. And with you as with us, your unpreparedness stands as your warrant before history, that not from American minds and wills came the provocation to this war.

But your actual and realised co-operation sets me on lines of thought that distract me, for the moment, from the first plan of this letter. The special Musketry School with which I had meant to open it, must wait till its close. I find my mind full instead—in connection with the news from Washington—of those recently issued War Office pamphlets of which I spoke in my last letter; and I propose to run through their story. These pamphlets, issued not for publication but for the information of those concerned, are the first frank record of *our national experience* in connection with the war; and for all your wonderful American resource and inventiveness, your American energy and wealth, you will certainly, as prudent men, make full use of our experience in the coming months.

Last year, for *England's Effort*, I tried vainly to collect some of these very facts and figures, which the War Office was still jealously—'and no doubt quite rightly—withholding. Now at last they are available, told by "authority," and one can hardly doubt that each of these passing days will give them—for America a double significance. Surpass the story, if you can; we shall bear you no grudge! But up till now, it remains a chapter unique in the history of war. Many Americans, as your original letter to me pointed out, had still, last year, practically no conception of what we were doing and had done. The majority of our own people, indeed, were in much the same case. While the great story was still in the making, while the foundations were still being laid, it was impossible to correct all the annoying underestimates, all the ignorant or careless judgments, of people who took a point for the whole. The men at the heart of things could only set their teeth, keep silence and give no information that could help the enemy. The battle of the Somme, last July, was the first real testing of their work. The Hindenburg retreat, the successes in Mesopotamia, the marvellous spectacle of the Armies in France—and before this letter could be sent to Press, the glorious news from the Arras front!—are the present fruits of it.

Like you, we had, at the outbreak of war, some 500,000 men, all told, of whom not half were fully trained. None of us British folk will ever forget the Rally of the First Hundred Thousand! On the 8th of August, four days after the Declaration of War, Lord Kitchener asked for them. He got them in a fortnight. But the stream rushed on—in the fifth week of the war alone 250,000 men enlisted; 30,000 recruits—the yearly number enlisted before the war—joined in one day. Within six or seven weeks the half-million available at the beginning of the war had been *more than doubled.*

Then came a pause. The War Office, snowed under, not knowing where to turn for clothes, boots, huts, rifles, guns, ammunition, tried to check the stream by raising the recruits' standards. A mistake!—but soon recognised. In another month, under the influence of the victory on the Marne, and while the Germans were preparing the attacks on the British Line so miraculously beaten off in the first battle of Ypres, the momentary check had been lost in a fresh outburst of national energy. You will remember how the Parliamentary Recruiting Committee came into being, that first autumn?—how the Prime Minister took the lead, and the two great political parties of the country agreed to bring all their organisation, central or local, to bear on the supreme question of getting men for the Army. Tory and Radical toured the country together. The hottest opponents stood on the same platform. *L'union sacrée*—to use the French phrase, so vivid and so true, by which our great Ally has charmed her own discords to rest in defence of the country—became a reality here too, in spite of strikes, in spite of Ireland.

By July 1915—the end of the first year of war—more than 2,000,000 men had voluntarily enlisted. But the military chiefs knew well that it was but a half-way house. They knew, too, that it was not enough to get men and rush them out to the trenches as soon as any kind of training could be given them. The available men must be sorted out. Some, indeed, must be brought back from the fighting line for work as vital as the fighting itself.

So Registration came—the first real step towards organising the nation. 150,000 voluntary workers helped to register all men and women in the country, from eighteen to sixty-five, and on the results Lord Derby built his group system, which *almost* enabled us to do without compulsion. Between October and December 1915, another two million and a quarter men had "attested"—that is, had pledged themselves to come up for training when called on.

But, as every observer of this new England knows, we have here less than half the story. From a nation not invaded, protected, on the contrary, by its sea ramparts from the personal cruelties and ravages of war, to gather in between four and five million voluntary recruits was a great achievement. But to turn these recruits at the shortest possible notice, under the hammer-blows of a war, in which our enemies had every initial advantage, into armies equipped and trained according to modern standards, might well have seemed to those who undertook it an impossible task. And the task had to be accomplished, the riddle solved, before, in the face of the enemy, the incredible difficulties of it could possibly be admitted. The creators of the new armies worked, as far as they could, behind a screen. But now the screen is down, and we are allowed to see their difficulties in their true perspective—as they existed during the first months of the war.

In the first place—accommodation! At the opening of war we had barrack-room for 176,000 men. What to do with these capped, bare-headed, or straw-hatted multitudes who poured in at Lord Kitchener's call! They were temporarily housed—somehow—under every kind of shelter. But military huts for half a million men were immediately planned—then for nearly a million.

Timber—labour—lighting—water—drainage—roads—everything, had to be provided, and was provided. Billeting filled up the gaps, and large camps were built by private enterprise to be taken in time by the Government. Of course mistakes were made. Of course there were some dishonest contractors and some incompetent officials. But the breath, the winnowing blast of the national need was behind it all. By the end of the first year of war, the "problem of quartering the troops in the chief training centres had been solved."

In the next place, there were no clothes. A dozen manufacturers of khaki cloth existed before the war. They had to be pushed up as quickly as possible to 200. Which of us in the country districts does not remember the blue emergency suits, of which a co-operative society was able by a lucky stroke to provide 400,000 for the new recruits?—or the other motley coverings of the hosts that drilled in our fields and marched about our lanes? The War Office Notes, under my hand, speak of these months as the "tatterdemalion stage." For what clothes and boots there were must go to the men at the Front, and the men at home had just to take their chance.

Well! It took a year and five months—breathless months of strain and stress— while Germany was hammering East and West on the long-drawn lines of the Allies. But by then, January 1916, the Army was not only clothed, housed, and very largely armed, but we were manufacturing for our Allies.

As to the arms and equipment, look back at these facts. When the Expeditionary Force had taken its rifles abroad in August 1914, 150,000 rifles were left in the country, and many of them required to be resighted. The few Service rifles in each battalion were handed round "as the Three Fates handed round their one eye, in the story of Perseus"; old rifles, and inferior rifles "technically known as D.P.," were eagerly made use of. But after seven months' hard training with nothing better than these makeshifts, "men were apt to get depressed."

It was just the same with the Artillery. At the outbreak of war we had guns for eight divisions—say 140,000 men. And there was no plant wherewith to make and keep up more than that supply. Yet guns had to be sent as fast as they could be made to France, Egypt, Gallipoli. How were the gunners at home to be trained?

It was done, so to speak, with blood and tears. For seven months it was impossible for the gunner in training even to see, much less to work or fire the gun to which he was being trained. Zealous officers provided dummy wooden guns for their men. All kinds of devices were tried. And even when the guns themselves arrived, they came often without the indispensable accessories—range-finders, directors, and the like.

It was a time of hideous anxiety for both Government and War Office. For the military history of 1915 was largely a history of shortage of guns and ammunition—whether on the Western or Eastern fronts. All the same, by the end of 1915 the thing was in hand. The shells from the new factories were arriving in ever-increasing volume; and the guns were following.

In a chapter of *England's Effort* I have described the amazing development of some of the great armament works in order to meet this cry for guns, as I saw it in February 1916. The second stage of the war had then begun. The first was over, and we were steadily overtaking our colossal task. The Somme proved it abundantly. But the expansion *still* goes on; and what the nation owes to the directing brains and ceaseless energy of these nominally private but really national firms has never been sufficiently recognised. On my writing-desk is a letter received, not many days ago, from a world-famous firm whose works I saw last year: "Since your visit here in the early part of last year, there have been very large additions to the works." Buildings to accommodate new aeroplane and armament construction of different kinds are mentioned, and the letter continues: "We have also put up another gun-shop, 565 feet long, and 163 feet wide—in three extensions—of which the third is nearing completion. These additions are all to increase the output of guns. The value of that output is now 60 per cent, greater than it was in 1915. In the last twelve months, the output of shells has been one and a half times more than it was in the previous year." No wonder that the humane director who writes speaks with keen sympathy of the "long-continued strain" upon masters and men. But he adds—"When we all feel it, we think of our soldiers and sailors, doing their duty—unto death."

And then—to repeat—if the *difficulties of equipment* were huge, they were almost as nothing to the *difficulties of training*. The facts as the War Office has now revealed them (the latest of these most illuminating brochures is dated April 2nd, 1917) are almost incredible. It will be an interesting time when our War Office and yours come to compare notes!—"when Peace has calmed the world." For you are now facing the same grim task—how to find the shortest cuts to the making of an Army—which confronted us in 1914.

In the first place, what military trainers there were in the country had to be sent abroad with the first Expeditionary Force. Adjutants, N.C.O.'s, all the experienced pilots in the Flying Corps, nearly all the qualified instructors in physical training, the vast majority of all the seasoned men in every branch of the Service—down, as I have said, to the Army cooks—departed overseas. At the very last moment an officer or two were shed from every battalion of the

Expeditionary Force to train those left behind. Even so, there was "hardly even a nucleus of experts left." And yet—officers for 500,000 men had to be found—*within a month*—from August 4th, 1914.

How was it done? The War Office answer makes fascinating reading. The small number of regular officers left behind—200 officers of the Indian Army—retired officers, "dug-outs"—all honour to them!—wounded officers from the Front; all were utilised. But the chief sources of supply, as we all know, were the Officers' Training Corps at the Universities and Public Schools which we owe to the divination, the patience, the hard work of Lord Haldane. *Twenty thousand potential officers were supplied* by the O.T.C's. What should we have done without them?

But even so, there was no time to train them in the practical business of war—and such a war! Yet *their* business was to train recruits, while they themselves were untrained. At first, those who were granted "temporary commissions" were given a month's training. Then even that became impossible. During the latter months of 1914 "there was practically no special training given to infantry subalterns, with temporary commissions." With 1915, the system of a month's training was revived—pitifully little, yet the best that could be done. But during the first five months of the war most of the infantry subalterns of the new armies "had to train themselves as best they could in the intervals of training their men."

One's pen falters over the words. Before the inward eye rises the phantom host of these boy-officers who sprang to England's aid in the first year of the war, and whose graves lie scattered in an endless series along the western front and on the heights of Gallipoli. Without counting the cost for a moment, they came to the call of the Great Mother, from near and far. "They trained themselves, while they were training their men." Not for them the plenty of guns and shells that now at least lessens the hideous sacrifice that war demands; not for them the many protective devices and safeguards that the war itself has developed. Their young bodies—their precious lives—paid the price. And in the Mother-heart of England they lie—gathered and secure—for ever.

* * * * *

But let me go a little further with the new War Office facts.

The year 1915 saw great and continuous advance. During that year, an *average number of over a million troops* were being trained in the United Kingdom, apart from the armies abroad. The First, Second, and Third Armies naturally came off much better than the Fourth and Fifth, who were yet being recruited all the time. What equipment, clothes and arms there were the first three armies got; the rest had to wait. But all the same, the units of these later armies were doing the best they could for themselves all the time; nobody stood still. And gradually—surely—order was evolved out of the original chaos. The Army Orders of the past had dropped out of sight with the beginning of the war. Everything had to be planned anew. The one governing factor was the "necessity of getting men to the front at the earliest possible moment." Six months' courses were laid down for all arms. It was very rare, however, that any course could be strictly carried out, and after the first three armies, the training of the rest seemed, for a time, to be all beginnings!—with the final stage farther and farther away. And always the same difficulty of guns, rifles, huts, and the rest.

But, like its own tanks, the War Office went steadily on, negotiating one obstacle after another. Special courses for special subjects began to be set up. Soon artillery officers had no longer to join their batteries *at once* on appointment; R.E. officers could be given a seven weeks' training at Chatham; little enough, "for a man supposed to know the use and repairs of telephones and telegraphs, or the way to build or destroy a bridge, or how to meet the countless other needs with which a sapper is called upon to deal!" Increasing attention was paid to staff training and staff courses. And insufficient as it all was, for months, the general results of this haphazard training, when the men actually got into the field—all short-comings and disappointments admitted—were nothing short of wonderful. Had the Germans forgotten that we are and always have been a fighting people? That fact, at any rate, was brought home to them by the unbroken spirit of the troops who held the line in France and Flanders in 1915 against all attempts to break through; and at Neuve Chapelle, or Loos, or a hundred other minor engagements, only wanted numbers and ammunition—above all ammunition!—to win them the full victory they had rightly earned.

Of this whole earlier stage, the *junior subaltern* was the leading figure. It was he—let me insist upon it anew—whose spirit made the new armies. If the tender figure of the "*Lady of the Lamp*" has become for many of us the chief symbol of the Crimean struggle, when Britain comes to embody in sculpture or in painting that which has touched her most deeply in this war, she will choose—surely—the figure of a boy of nineteen, laughing, eager, undaunted, as quick to die as to live, carrying in his young hands the "Luck" of England.

* * * * *

But with the end of 1915, the first stage, the elementary stage, of the new Armies came to an end. When I stood, in March 1916, on the Scherpenberg hill, looking out over the Salient, new conditions reigned. The Officer Cadet Corps had been formed; a lively and continuous intercourse between the realities of the front and the training at home had been set up; special schools in all subjects of military interest had been founded, often, as we have seen, by the zeal of individual officers, to be then gradually incorporated in the Army system. Men insufficiently trained in the early months had been given the opportunity—which they eagerly took—of beginning at the beginning again, correcting mistakes and incorporating all the latest knowledge. Even a lieutenant-colonel, before commanding a battalion, could go to school once more; and even for officers and men "in rest," there were, and are, endless opportunities of seeing and learning, which few wish to forgo.

And that brings me to what is now shaping itself—the final result. The year just passed, indeed—from March to March—has practically rounded our task—though the "learning" of the Army is never over!—and has seen the transformation—whether temporary or permanent, who yet can tell?—of the England of 1914, with its zealous mobs of untrained and "tatterdemalion" recruits, into a great military power,[This letter was finished just as the news of the Easter Monday Battle of Arras was coming in.] disposing of armies in no whit inferior to those of Germany, and bringing to bear upon the science of war—now that Germany has forced us to it—the best intelligence, and the best *character*, of the nation. The most insolent of the German military newspapers are already bitterly confessing it.

* * * * *

My summary—short and imperfect as it is—of this first detailed account of its work which the War Office has allowed to be made public—has carried me far afield.

The motor has been waiting long at the door of the hospitable headquarters which have entertained us! Let me return to it, to the great spectacle of the present—after this retrospect of the Past.

Again the crowded roads—the young and vigorous troops—the manifold sights illustrating branch after branch of the Army. I recall a draft, tired with marching, clambering with joy into some empty lorries, and sitting there peacefully content, with legs dangling and the ever blessed cigarette for company, then an aeroplane station—then a football field, with a violent game going on—a Casualty Clearing Station, almost a large hospital—another football match!—a battery of eighteen-pounders on the march, and beyond an old French market town crowded with lorries and men. In the midst of it D—— suddenly draws my attention to a succession of great nozzles passing us, with their teams and limbers. I have stood beside the forging and tempering of their brothers in the gun-shops of the north, have watched the testing and callipering of their shining throats. They are 6-inch naval guns on their way to the line—like everything else, part of the storm to come.

And in and out, among the lorries and the guns, stream the French folk, women, children, old men, alert, industrious, full of hope, with friendly looks for their Allies. Then the town passes, and we are out again in the open country, leaving the mining village behind. We are not very far at this point from that portion of the line which I saw last year under General X's guidance. But everything looks very quiet and rural, and when we emerged on the high ground of the school we had come to see, I might have imagined myself on a Surrey or Hertfordshire common. The officer in charge, a "mighty hunter" in civil life, showed us his work with a quiet but most contagious enthusiasm. The problem that he, and his colleagues engaged in similar work in other sections of the front, had to solve, was—how to beat the Germans at their own game of "sniping," which cost us so many lives in the first year and a half of war; in other words, how to train a certain number of men to an art of rifle-shooting, combining the instincts and devices of a "Pathfinder" with the subtleties of modern optical and mechanical science. "Don't think of this as meant primarily to kill," says the Chief of the School, as he walks beside me—"it is meant primarily to *protect*. We lost our best men—young and promising officers in particular—by the score before we learnt the tricks of the German 'sniper' and how to meet them." German "sniping," as our guide explains, is by no means all tricks. For the most part, it means just first-rate shooting, combined with the trained instinct and *flair* of the sportsman. Is there anything that England—and Scotland—should provide more abundantly? Still, there are tricks, and our men have learnt them.

26

Of the many surprises of the school I may not now speak. Above all, it is a school of *observation*. Nothing escapes the eye or the ear. Every point, for instance, connected with our two unfamiliar figures will have been elaborately noted by those men on the edge of the hill; the officer in charge will presently get a careful report on us.

"We teach our men the old great game of war—wit against wit—courage against courage—life against life. We try many men here, and reject a good few. But the men who have gone through our training here are valuable, both for attack and defence—above all, let me repeat it, they are valuable for *protection*."

And what is meant by this, I have since learnt in greater detail. Before these schools were started, *every day* saw a heavy toll—especially of officers' lives—taken by German snipers. Compare with this one of the latest records: that out of fifteen battalions there were only nine men killed by snipers *in three months.*

We leave the hill, half sliding down the frozen watercourse that leads to it, and are in the motor again, bound for an Army Headquarters.

No. 4

April 14th, 1917.

DEAR MR. ROOSEVELT,—As the news comes flashing in, these April days, and all the world holds its breath to hear the latest messages from Arras and the Vimy ridge, it is natural that in the memory of a woman who, six weeks ago, was a spectator—before the curtain rose—of the actual scene of such events, every incident and figure of that past experience, as she looks back upon it, should gain a peculiar and shining intensity.

The battle of the Vimy Ridge [*April 8th*] is clearly going to be the second (the first was the German retreat on the Somme) of those "decisive events" determining this year the upshot of the war, to which the Commander-in-Chief, with so strong and just a confidence, directed the eyes of this country some three months ago. When I was in the neighbourhood of the great battlefield—one may say it now!—the whole countryside was one vast preparation. The signs of the coming attack were everywhere—troops, guns, ammunition, food dumps, hospitals, air stations—every actor and every property in the vast and tragic play were on the spot, ready for the moment and the word.

Yet, except in the Headquarters and Staff Councils of the Army nobody knew when the moment and the word would come, and nobody spoke of them. The most careful and exact organisation for the great movement was going on. No visitor would hear anything of it. Only the nameless stir in the air, the faces of officers at Headquarters, the general alacrity, the endless *work* everywhere, prophesied the great things ahead. Perpetual, highly organised, scientific drudgery is three parts of war, it seems, as men now wage it. The Army, as I saw it, was at work—desperately at work!—but "dreaming on things to come."

One delightful hour of that March day stands out for me in particular. The strong, attractive presence of an Army Commander, whose name will be for ever linked with that of the battle of the Vimy ridge, surrounded by a group of distinguished officers; a long table, and a too brief stay; conversation that carries for me the thrill of the *actual thing*, close by, though it may not differ very much

27

from wartalk at home: these are the chief impressions that remain. The General beside me, with that look in his kind eyes which seems to tell of nights shortened by hard work, says a few quietly confident things about the general situation, and then we discuss a problem which one of the party—not a soldier—starts.

Is it true or untrue that long habituation to the seeing or inflicting of pain and death, that the mere sights and sounds of the trenches tend with time to brutalise men, and will make them callous when they return to civil life? Do men grow hard and violent in this furnace after a while, and will the national character suffer thereby in the future? The General denies it strongly. "I see no signs of it. The kindness of the men to each other, to the wounded, whether British or German, to the French civilians, especially the women and children, is as marked as it ever was. It is astonishing the good behaviour of the men in these French towns; it is the rarest thing in the world to get a complaint."

I ask for some particulars of the way in which the British Army "runs" the French towns and villages in our zone. How is it done? "It is all summed up in three words," says an officer present, "M. le Maire!" What we should have done without the local functionaries assigned by the French system to every village and small town it is hard to say. They are generally excellent people; they have the confidence of their fellow townsmen, and know everything about them. Our authorities on taking over a town or village do all the preliminaries through M. le Maire, and all goes well.

The part played, indeed, by these local chiefs of the civil population throughout France during the war has been an honourable and arduous—in many cases a tragic—one. The murder, under the forms of a court-martial, of the Maire of Senlis and his five fellow hostages stands out among the innumerable German cruelties as one of peculiar horror. Everywhere in the occupied departments the Maire has been the surety for his fellows, and the Germans have handled them often as a cruel boy torments some bird or beast he has captured, for the pleasure of showing his power over it.

From the wife of the Maire of an important town in Lorraine I heard the story of how her husband had been carried off as a hostage for three weeks, while the Germans were in occupation. Meanwhile German officers were billeted in her charming old house. "They used to say to me every day with great politeness that they *hoped* my husband would not be shot. 'But why should he be shot, monsieur? He will do nothing to deserve it.' On which they would shrug their shoulders and say, 'Madame, c'est la guerre!' evidently wishing to see me terrified. But I never gave them that pleasure."

A long drive home, through the dark and silent country. Yet everywhere one feels the presence of the Army. We draw up to look at a sign-post at some cross roads by the light of one of the motor lamps. Instantly a couple of Tommies emerge from the darkness and give help. In passing through a village a gate suddenly opens and a group of horses comes out, led by two men in khaki; or from a Y.M.C.A. hut laughter and song float out into the night. And soon in these farms and cottages everybody will be asleep under the guard of the British Forces, while twenty miles away, in the darkness, the guns we saw in the morning are endlessly harassing and scourging the enemy lines, preparing for the day when the thoughts now maturing in the minds of the Army leaders will leap in flame to light.

* * * * *

To-day we are off for the Somme. I looked out anxiously with the dawn, and saw streaks of white mist lying over the village and the sun struggling through. But as we start on the road to Amiens, the mist gains the upper hand, and we begin to be afraid that we shall not get any of those wide views from the west of Albert over the Somme country which are possible in clear weather. Again the high upland, and this time *three* tanks on the road, but motionless, alack! the nozzles of their machine guns just visible on their great sides. Then a main road, if it can be called a road since the thaw has been at work upon it. Every mile or two, as our chauffeur explains, the pavé "is all burst up" from below, and we rock and lunge through holes and ruts that only an Army motor can stand. But German prisoners are thick on the worst bits, repairing as hard as they can. Was it perhaps on some of these men that certain of the recent letters that are always coming into G.H.Q. have been found? I will quote a few of those which have not yet seen the light.

Here are a batch of letters written in January of this year from Hamburg and its neighbourhood:

"It is indeed a miserable existence. How will it all end? There is absolutely nothing to be got here. Honey costs *6s. 6d.* a pound, goose fat *18s.* a pound. Lovely prices, aren't they? One cannot do much by way of heating, as there is no coal. We can just freeze and starve at home. Everybody is ill. All the infirmaries are overflowing. Small-pox has broken out. You are being shot at the front, and at home we are gradually perishing."

" … On the Kaiser's birthday, military bands played everywhere. When one passes and listens to this tomfoolery, and sees the emaciated and overworked men in war-time, swaying to the sounds of music, and enjoying it, one's very gall rises. Why music? Of course, if times were different, one could enjoy music. But to-day! It should be the aim of the higher authorities to put an end to this murder. In every sound of music the dead cry for revenge. I can assure you that it is very surprising that there has not been a single outbreak here, but it neither can nor will last much longer. How can a human being subsist on 1/4 lb. of potatoes a day? I should very much like the Emperor to try and live for a week on the fare we get. He would then say it is impossible…. I heard something this week quite unexpectedly, which although I had guessed it before, yet has depressed me still more. However, we will hope for the best."

"You write to say that you are worse off than a beast of burden…. I couldn't send you any cakes, as we had no more flour…. We have abundant bread tickets. From Thursday to Saturday I can still buy five loaves…. My health is bad; not my asthma, no, but my whole body is collapsing. We are all slowly perishing, and this is what it is all coming to."

" … The outlook here is also sad. One cannot get a bucket of coal. The stores and dealers have none. The schools are closing, as there is no coal. Soon everybody will be in the same plight. Neither coal nor vegetables can be bought. Holland is sending us nothing more, and we have none. We get 3-1/2 lb. of potatoes per person. In the next few days we shall only have swedes to eat, which must be dried."

* * * * *

A letter written from Hamburg in February, and others from Coblenz are tragic reading:

" ... We shall soon have nothing more to eat. We earn no money, absolutely none; it is sad but true. Many people are dying here from inanition or under-feeding."

Or, take these from Neugersdorf, in Saxony:

"We cannot send you any butter, for we have none to eat ourselves. For three weeks we have not been able to get any potatoes. So we only have turnips to eat, and now there are no more to be had. We do not know what we can get for dinner this week, and if we settle to get our food at the Public Food-Kitchen we shall have to stand two hours for it."

"Here is February once more—one month nearer to peace. Otherwise all is the same. Turnips! Turnips! Very few potatoes, only a little bread, and no thought of butter or meat; on the other hand, any quantity of hunger. I understand your case is not much better on the Somme."

Or this from a man of the Ersatz Battalion, 19th F.A.R., Dresden:

"Since January 16th I have been called up and put into the Foot Artillery at Dresden. On the 16th we were first taken to the Quartermaster's Stores, where 2,000 of us had to stand waiting in the rain from 2.30 to 6.30.... On the 23rd I was transferred to the tennis ground. We are more than 100 men in one room. Nearly all of us have frozen limbs at present. The food, too, is bad; sometimes it cannot possibly be eaten. Our training also is very quick, for we are to go *into the field in six weeks*."

Or these from Itzehoe and Hanover:

"Could you get me some silk? It costs 8s. a metre here.... To-day, the 24th, all the shops were stormed for bread, and 1,000 loaves were stolen from the bakery. There were several other thousand in stock. In some shops the windows were smashed. In the grocers' shops the butter barrels were rolled into the street. There were soldiers in civilian dress. The Mayor wanted to hang them. There are no potatoes this week."

"To-day, the 27th, the bakers' shops in the —— Road were stormed.... This afternoon the butchers' shops are to be stormed."

"If only peace would come soon! We have been standing to for an alarm these last days, as the people here are storming all the bakers' shops. It is a semi-revolution. It cannot last much longer."

To such a pass have the Kaiser and the Junker party brought their countrymen! Here, no doubt, are some of the recipients of such letters among the peaceful working groups in shabby green-grey, scattered along the roads of France. As we pass, the German N.C.O. often looks up to salute the officer who is with us, and the general aspect of the men—at any rate of the younger men—is cheerfully phlegmatic. At least they are safe from the British guns, and at least they have enough to eat. As to this, let me quote, by way of contrast, a few passages from letters written by prisoners in a British camp to their people at home. One might feel a quick pleasure in the creature-comfort they express but for the burning memory of our own prisoners, and the way in which thousands of them have been cruelly ill-treated, tormented even, in Germany—worst of all, perhaps, by German women.

The extracts are taken from letters written mostly in December and January last:

(*a*) " ... Dear wife, don't fret about me, because the English treat us very well. Only our own officers (N.C.O.'s) treat us even worse than they do at home in barracks; but that we're accustomed to...."

(*b*) " ... I'm now a prisoner in English hands, and I'm quite comfortable and content with my lot, for most of my comrades are dead. The English treat us well, and everything that is said to the contrary is not true. Our food is good. There are no meatless days, but we haven't any cigars...."

(*c*) Written from hospital, near Manchester: " ... I've been a prisoner since October, 1916. I'm extremely comfortable here.... Considering the times, I really couldn't wish you all anything better than to be here too!"

(*d*) " ... I am afraid I'm not in a position to send you very detailed letters about my life at present, but I can tell you that I am quite all right and comfortable, and that I wish every English prisoner were the same. Our new Commandant is very humane—strict, but just. You can tell everybody who thinks differently that I shall always be glad to prove that he is wrong...."

(*e*) " ... I suppose you are all thinking that we are having a very bad time here as prisoners. It's true we have to do without a good many things, but that after all one must get accustomed to. The English are really good people, which I never would have believed before I was taken prisoner. They try all they can to make our lot easier for us, and you know there are a great many of us now. So don't be distressed for us...."

X is passed, a large and prosperous town, with mills in a hollow. We climb the hill beyond it, and are off on a long and gradual descent to Amiens. This Picard country presents everywhere the same general features of rolling downland, thriving villages, old churches, comfortable country houses, straight roads, and well-kept woods. The battlefields of the Somme were once a continuation of it! But on this March day the uplands are wind-swept and desolate; and chilly white mists curl about them, with occasional bursts of pale sun.

Out of the mist there emerges suddenly an anti-aircraft section; then a great Army Service dump; and presently we catch sight of a row of hangars and the following notice, "Beware of aeroplanes ascending and descending across roads." For a time the possibility of charging into a biplane gives zest to our progress, as we fly along the road which cuts the aerodrome; but, alack! there are none visible and we begin to drop towards Amiens.

Then, outside the town, sentinels stop us, French and British; our passes are examined; and, under their friendly looks—betraying a little surprise!—we drive on into the old streets. I was in Amiens two years before the war, between trains, that I might refresh a somewhat faded memory of the cathedral. But not such a crowded, such a busy Amiens as this! The streets are so full that we have to turn out of the main street, directed by a French military policeman, and find our way by a détour to the cathedral.

As we pass through Amiens arrangements are going on for the "taking over" of another large section of the French line, south of Albert; as far, it is rumoured, as Roye and Lagny. At last, with our new armies, we can relieve more of the French divisions, who have borne so gallantly and for so many months the burden of their long line. It is true that the bulk of the German forces are massed against the British lines, and that in some parts of the centre and the east, owing to the nature of the ground, they are but thinly strung along the French front, which accounts partly for the disproportion in the number of kilometres covered by each Ally. But, also, we had to make our Army; the French, God be thanked, had theirs ready, and gloriously have they stood the brunt, as the defenders of civilisation, till we could take our full share.

And now we, who began with 45 kilometres of the battle-line, have gradually become responsible for 185, so that "at last," says a French friend to me in Paris, "our men can have a rest, some of them for the first time! And, by Heaven, they've earned it!"

Yet, in this "taking over" there are many feelings concerned. For the French *poilu* and our Tommy it is mostly the occasion for as much fraternisation as their fragmentary knowledge of each other's speech allows; the Frenchman is proud to show his line, the Britisher is proud to take it over; there are laughter and eager good will; on the whole, it is a red-letter day. But sometimes there strikes in a note "too deep for tears." Here is a fragment from an account of a "taking over," written by an eye-witness:

Trains of a prodigious length are crawling up a French railway. One follows so closely upon another that the rear truck of the first is rarely out of sight of the engine-driver of the second. These trains are full of British soldiers. Most of them are going to the front for the first time. They are seated everywhere, on the trucks, on the roof—legs dangling over the edge—inside, and even over the buffers. Presently they arrive at their goal. The men clamber out on to the siding, collect their equipment and are ready for a march up country. A few children run alongside them, shouting, "Anglais!" "Anglais!" And some of them take the soldiers' hands and walk on with them until they are tired.

Now the trenches are reached, and the men break into single file. But the occasion is not the usual one of taking over a few trenches. *We are relieving some sixty miles of French line.* There is, however, no confusion. The right men are sent to the right places, and everything is done quietly. It is like a great tide sweeping in, and another sweeping out. Sixty miles of trenches are gradually changing their nationality.

The German, a few yards over the way, knows quite well what is happening. A few extra shells whizz by; a trench mortar or two splutter a welcome; but it makes little difference to the weary German who mans the trenches over against him. Only, the new men are fresh and untired, and the German has no Ally who can give him corresponding relief.

It has all been so quietly done! Yet it is really a great moment. The store of man power which Great Britain possesses is beginning to take practical effect. The French, who held the long lines at the beginning of war, who stood before Verdun and threw their legions on the road to Péronne, are now being freed for work elsewhere. They have "carried on" till Great Britain was ready, and now she is ready.

* * * * *

This was more than the beginning of a new tour of duty [says another witness]. I felt the need of some ceremony, and I think others felt the need of it too. There were little half-articulate attempts, in the darkness, of men trying to show what they felt—a whisper or two—in the queer jargon that is growing up between the two armies. An English sentry mounted upon the fire-step, and looked out into the darkness beside the Frenchman, and then, before the Frenchman stepped down, patted him on the shoulder, as though he would say: "These trenches—*all right*!—we'll look after them!"

Then I stumbled into a dug-out. A candle burnt there, and a French officer was taking up his things. He nodded and smiled. "I go," he said. "I am not sorry, and yet——" He shrugged his shoulders. I understood. One is never sorry to go, but these trenches—these bits of France, where Frenchmen had died—would no longer be guarded by Frenchmen. Then he waved his hand round the little dug-out. "We give a little more of France into your keeping." His gesture was extravagant and light, but his face was grave as he said it. He turned and went out. I followed. He walked along the communication trench after his men, and I along the line of my silent sentries. I spoke to one or two, and then stood on the fire-step, looking out into the night. I had the Frenchman's words in my head: "We give a little more of France into your keeping!" It was not these trenches only, where I stood, but all that lay out there in the darkness, which had been given into our keeping. Its dangers were ours now. There were villages away there in the heart of the night, still unknown to all but the experts at home, whose names—like Thiepval and Bazentin—would soon be English names, familiar to every man in Britain as the streets of his own town. All this France had entrusted to our care this night.

Such were the scenes that were quietly going on, not much noticed by the public at home during the weeks of February and March, and such were the thoughts in men's minds. How plainly one catches through the words of the last speaker an eager prescience of events to come!—the sweep of General Gough on Warlencourt and Bapaume—the French reoccupation of Péronne.

One word for the cathedral of Amiens before we leave the bustling streets of the old Picard capital. This is so far untouched and unharmed, though exposed, like everything else behind the front, to the bombs of German aeroplanes. The

33

great west front has disappeared behind a mountain of sandbags; the side portals are protected in the same way, and inside, the superb carvings of the choir are buried out of sight. But at the back of the choir the famous weeping cherub sits weeping as before, peacefully querulous. There is something irritating in his placid and too artistic grief. Not so is "Rachel weeping for her children" in this war-ravaged country. Sterner images of Sorrow are wanted here—looking out through burning eyes for the Expiation to come.

* * * * *

Then we are off, bound for Albert, though first of all for the Headquarters of the particular Army which has this region in charge. The weather, alack! is still thick. It is under cover of such an atmosphere that the Germans have been stealing away, removing guns and stores wherever possible, and leaving rear-guards to delay our advance. But when the rear-guards amount to some 100,000 men, resistance is still formidable, not to be handled with anything but extreme prudence by those who have such vast interests in charge as the Generals of the Allies.

Our way takes us first through a small forest, where systematic felling and cutting are going on under British forestry experts. The work is being done by German prisoners, and we catch a glimpse through the trees of their camp of huts in a barbed-wire enclosure. Their guards sleep under canvas! ... And now we are in the main street of a large picturesque village, approaching a château. A motor lorry comes towards us, driven at a smart pace, and filled with grey-green uniforms. Prisoners!—this time fresh from the field. We have already heard rumours on our way of successful fighting to the south.

The famous Army Commander himself, who had sent us a kind invitation to lunch with him, is unexpectedly engaged in conference with a group of French generals; but there is a welcome suggestion that on our way back from the Somme he will be free and able to see me. Meanwhile we go off to luncheon and much talk with some members of the Staff in a house on the village street. Everywhere I notice the same cheerful, one might even say radiant, confidence. No boasting in words, but a conviction that penetrates through all talk that the tide has turned, and that, however long it may take to come fully up, it is we whom it is floating surely on to that fortune which is no blind hazard, but the child of high faith and untiring labour. Of that labour the Somme battlefields we were now to see will always remain in my mind—in spite of ruin, in spite of desolation—as a kind of parable in action, never to be forgotten.

No. 5

April 26th, 1917.

DEAR MR. ROOSEVELT,—Amid the rushing events of these days— America rousing herself like an eagle "with eyes intentive to bedare the sun"; the steady and victorious advance along the whole front in France, which day by day is changing the whole aspect of the war; the Balfour Mission; the signs of deep distress in Germany—it is sometimes difficult to throw oneself back into the mood of even six weeks ago! History is coming so fast off the loom! And yet six weeks ago I stood at the pregnant beginnings of it all, when, though nature in the bitter frost and slush of early March showed no signs of spring, the winter lull was over, and everywhere on the British front men knew that great things were stirring.

Before I reached G.H.Q., Field-Marshal Sir Douglas Haig had already reported the recapture or surrender of eleven villages on the Ancre during February, including Serre and Gommecourt, which had defied our efforts in the summer of 1916. That is to say, after three months of trench routine and trench endurance imposed by a winter which seemed to have let loose every possible misery of cold and wet, of storm and darkness, on the fighting hosts in France, the battle of the Somme had moved steadily forward again from the point it had reached in November. Only, when the curtain rose on the new scene it was found that during these three months strange things had been happening.

About the middle of November, after General Gough's brilliant strokes on the Ancre, which gave us St. Pierre Divion, Beaucourt, and Beaumont Hamel, and took us up to the outskirts of Grandcourt, the *Frankfurter Zeitung* wrote—"For us Germans the days of the crisis on the Somme are over. Let the French and English go on sacrificing the youth of their countries here. They will not thereby achieve anything more." Yet when this was written the German Higher Command was already well aware that the battle of the Somme had been won by the Allies, and that it would be impossible for Germany to hold out on the same ground against another similar attack.

Three months, however, of an extraordinarily hard winter gave them a respite, and enabled them to veil the facts from their own people. The preparations for retirement, which snow and fog and the long nights of January helped them to conceal in part from our Air Service, must have actually begun not many weeks after General Gough's last successes on the Ancre, when the British advance paused, under stress of weather, before Grandcourt and Bapaume. So that in the latter half of February, when General Gough again pushed forward, it was to feel the German line yielding before him; and by March 3rd, the day of my visit to the Somme, it was only a question of how far the Germans would go and what the retreat meant.

Meanwhile, in another section of the line our own plans were maturing, which were to bear fruit five weeks later in the brilliant capture of that Vimy ridge I had seen on March 2, filling the blue middle distance, from the bare upland of Notre Dame de Lorette. If on the Somme the anvil was to some extent escaping from the hammer, in the coming battle of Arras the hammer was to take its full revenge.

These things, however, were still hidden from all but the few, and in the first days of March the Germans had not yet begun to retire in front of the French line further south. The Somme advance was still the centre of things, and Bapaume had not yet fallen. As we drove on towards Albert we knew that we should be soon close behind our own guns, and within range of the enemy's.

No one who has seen it in war-time will ever forget the market-place of Albert—the colossal heaps of wreck that fill the centre of it; the new, pretentious church, rising above the heaps, a brick-and-stucco building of the worst neo-

Catholic taste, which has been so gashed and torn and broken, while still substantially intact, that all its mean and tawdry ornament has disappeared in a certain strange dignity of ruin; and last, the hanging Virgin, holding up the Babe above the devastation below, in dumb protest to God and man. The gilded statue, which now hangs at right angles to the tower, has, after its original collapse under shell-fire, been fixed in this position by the French Engineers; and it is to be hoped that when the church comes to be rebuilt the figure will be left as it is. There is something extraordinarily significant and dramatic in its present attitude. Whatever artistic defects the statue may have are out of sight, and it seems as it hangs there, passionately hovering, above the once busy centre of a prosperous town, to be the very symbol and voice of France calling the world to witness.

A few more minutes, and we are through the town, moving slowly along the Albert-Bapaume road, that famous road which will be a pilgrims' way for generations to come.

"To other folk," writes an officer quoted by Mr. Buchan in his *Battle of the Somme*, "and on the maps, one place seems just like another, I suppose; but to us—La Boisselle and Ovillers—my hat!"

To walk about in those hells! I went along the "sunken road" all the way to Contalmaison. Talk about sacred ground! The new troops coming up now go barging across in the most light-hearted way. It means no more to them than the roads behind used to mean to us. But when I think how we watered every yard of it with blood and sweat! Children might play there now, if it didn't look so like the aftermath of an earthquake. I have a sort of feeling it ought to be marked off somehow, a permanent memorial.

The same emotion as that which speaks in this letter—so far, at least, as it can be shared by those who had no part in the grim scene itself—held us, the first women-pilgrims to tread these roads and trampled slopes since the battle-storm of last autumn passed over them. The sounds of an immortal host seemed to rush past us on the air—mingled strangely with the memory of hot July days in an English garden far away, when the news of the great advance came thundering in hour by hour.

"The aftermath of an earthquake!" Do the words express the reality before us as we move along the mile of road between Albert and La Boisselle? Hardly. The earth-shudder that visits a volcanic district may topple towns and villages into ruins in a few minutes. It does not tear and grind and pound what it has overturned, through hour after hour, till there is nothing left but mud and dust.

Not only all vegetation, but all the natural surface of the ground here has gone; and the villages are churned into the soil, as though some "hundred-handed Gyas" had been mixing and kneading them into a devil's dough. There are no continuous shell-holes, as we had expected to see. Those belong to the ground further up the ridge, where fourteen square miles are so closely shell-pocked that one can hardly drive a stake between the holes. But here on the way to La Boisselle and Contalmaison there is just the raw tumbled earth, from which all the natural covering of grass and trees and all the handiwork of man have been stripped and torn and hammered away, so that it has become a great dark wound on the countryside.

Suddenly we see gaping lines of old trenches rising on either side of the road, the white chalk of the subsoil marking their course. "British!" says the officer in front—who was himself in the battle. Only a few steps further on, as it seems, we come to the remains of the German front line, and the motor pauses while we try to get our bearings. There to the south, on our right, and curving eastward, are two trench lines perfectly clear still on the brown desolation, the British and the enemy front lines. From that further line, at half-past seven on the summer morning for ever blazoned in the annals of our people, the British Army went over the parapet, to gather in the victory prepared for it by the deadly strength and accuracy of British guns; made possible in its turn by the labour in far-off England of millions of workers—men and women—on the lathes and in the filling factories of these islands.

We move on up the road. Now we are among what remains of the trenches and dug-outs described in Sir Douglas Haig's despatch. "During nearly two years' preparations the enemy had spared no pains to render these defences impregnable," says the Commander-in-Chief; and he goes on to describe the successive lines of deep trenches, the bomb-proof shelters, and the wire entanglements with which the war correspondence of the winter has made us at home—on paper—so familiar. "The numerous woods and villages had been turned into veritable fortresses." The deep cellars in the villages, the pits and quarries of a chalk country, provided cover for machine guns and trench mortars. The dug-outs were often two storeys deep, "and connected by passages as much as thirty feet below the surface of the ground." Strong redoubts, mine-fields, concrete gun emplacements—everything that the best brains of the German Army could devise for our destruction—had been lavished on the German lines. And behind the first line was a second—and behind the second line a third. And now here we stand in the midst of what was once so vast a system. What remains of it—and of all the workings of the German mind that devised it? We leave the motor and go to look into the dug-outs which line the road, out of which the dazed and dying Germans flung themselves at the approach of our men after the bombardment, and then Captain F. guides us a little further to a huge mine crater, and we sink into the mud which surrounds it, while my eyes look out over what once was Ovillers, northward towards Thiépval, and the slopes behind which runs the valley of the Ancre; up and over this torn and naked land, where the new armies of Great Britain, through five months of some of the deadliest fighting known to history, fought their way yard by yard, ridge after ridge, mile after mile, caring nothing for pain, mutilation and death so that England and the cause of the Allies might live.

"*There were no stragglers, none!*" Let us never forget that cry of exultant amazement wrung from the lips of an eye-witness, who saw the young untried troops go over the parapet in the July dawn and disappear into the hell beyond. And there in the packed graveyards that dot these slopes lie thousands of them in immortal sleep; and as the Greeks in after days knew no nobler oath than that which pledged a man by those who fell at Marathon, so may the memory of those who fell here burn ever in the heart of England, a stern and consecrating force.

"Life is but the pebble sunk,
Deeds the circle growing!"

And from the deeds done on this hillside, the suffering endured, the life given up, the victory won, by every kind and type of man within the British State— rich and poor, noble and simple, street-men from British towns, country-men from British villages, men from Canadian prairies, from Australian and New Zealand homesteads—one has a vision, as one looks on into the future, of the impulse given here spreading out through history, unquenched and imperishable. The fight is not over—the victory is not yet—but on the Somme no English or French heart can doubt the end.

The same thoughts follow one along the sunken road to Contalmaison. Here, first, is the cemetery of La Boisselle, this heaped confusion of sandbags, of broken and overturned crosses, of graves tossed into a common ruin. And a little further are the ruins of Contalmaison, where the 3rd Division of the Prussian Guards was broken and 700 of them taken prisoners. Terrible are the memories of Contalmaison! Recall one letter only!—the letter written by a German soldier the day before the attack: "Nothing comes to us—no letters. The English keep such a barrage on our approaches—it is horrible. To-morrow morning it will be seven days since this bombardment began; we cannot hold out much longer. Everything is shot to pieces." And from another letter: "Every one of us in these five days has become years older—we hardly know ourselves."

It was among these intricate remains of trenches and dug-outs, round the fragments of the old chateau, that such things happened. Here, and among those ghastly fragments of shattered woods that one sees to south and east—Mametz, Trônes, Delville, High Wood—human suffering and heroism, human daring and human terror, on one side and on the other, reached their height. For centuries after the battle of Marathon sounds of armed men and horses were heard by night; and to pry upon that sacred rendezvous of the souls of the slain was frowned on by the gods. Only the man who passed through innocently and ignorantly, not knowing where he was, could pass through safely. And here also, in days to come, those who visit these spots in mere curiosity, as though they were any ordinary sight, will visit them to their hurt.

* * * * *

So let the first thoughts run which are evolved by this brown and torn devastation. But the tension naturally passes, and one comes back, first, to the *victory*—to the results of all that hard and relentless fighting, both for the British and the French forces, on this memorable battlefield north and south of the Somme. Eighty thousand prisoners, between five and six hundred guns of different calibres, and more than a thousand machine guns, had fallen to the Allies in four months and a half. Many square miles of French territory had been recovered. Verdun—glorious Verdun—had been relieved. Italy and Russia had been helped by the concentration of the bulk of the German forces on the Western front. The enemy had lost at least half a million men; and the Allied loss, though great, had been substantially less. Our new armies had gloriously proved themselves, and the legend of German invincibility was gone.

So much for the first-fruits. The *ultimate results* are only now beginning to appear in the steady retreat of German forces, unable to stand another attack, on the same line, now that the protection of the winter pause is over. "How far are we from our guns?" I ask the officer beside me. And, as I speak, a flash to the north-east on the higher ground towards Pozières lights up the grey distance. My companion measures the hillside with his eyes. "About 1,000 yards." Their objective now is a temporary German line in front of Bapaume. But we shall be in Bapaume in a few days. And then?

Death—Victory—Work; these are the three leading impressions that rise and take symbolic shape amid these scenes. Let me turn now to the last. For anyone with the common share of heart and imagination, the first thought here must be of the dead—the next, of swarming life. For these slopes and roads and ruins are again alive with men. Thousands and thousands of our soldiers are here, many of them going up to or coming back from the line, while others are working—working—incessantly at all that is meant by "advance" and "consolidation."

The transformation of a line of battle into an efficient "back of the Army" requires, it seems, an amazing amount of human energy, contrivance, and endurance. And what we see now is, of course, a second or third stage. First of all there is the "clearing up" of the actual battlefield. For this the work of the men now at work here—R.E.'s and Labour battalions—is too skilled and too valuable. It is done by fatigues and burying parties from the battalions in occupation of each captured section. The dead are buried; the poor human fragments that remain are covered with chlorate of lime; equipments of all kinds, the litter of the battlefield, are brought back to the salvage dumps, there to be sorted and sent back to the bases for repairs.

Then—or simultaneously—begins the work of the Engineers and the Labour men. Enough ground has to be levelled and shell-holes filled up for the driving through of new roads and railways, and the provision of places where tents, huts, dumps, etc., are to stand. Roughly speaking, I see, as I look round me, that a great deal of this work is here already far advanced. There are hundreds of men, carts, and horses at work on the roads, and everywhere one sees the signs of new railway lines, either of the ordinary breadth, or of the narrow gauges needed for the advanced carriage of food and ammunition. Here also is a great encampment of Nissen huts; there fresh preparations for a food or an ammunition dump.

With one pair of eyes one can only see a fraction of what is in truth going on. But the whole effect is one of vast and increasing industry, of an intensity of determined effort, which thrills the mind hardly less than the thought of the battle-line itself. "Yes, war *is* work," writes an officer who went through the Somme fighting, "much more than it is fighting. This is one of the surprises that the New Army soldiers find out here." Yet for the hope of the fighting moment men will go cheerfully through any drudgery, in the long days before and after; and when the fighting comes, will bear themselves to the wonder of the world.

On we move, slowly, towards Fricourt, the shattered remnants of the Mametz wood upon our left. More graveyards, carefully tended; spaces of peace amid the universal movement. And always, on the southern horizon, those clear lines of British trenches, whence sprang on July 1st, 1916, the irresistible attack on Montauban and Mametz. Suddenly, over the desolate ground to the west, we see a man hovering in mid-air, descending on a parachute from a captive balloon that seems to have suffered mishap. The small wavering object comes slowly down; we cannot see the landing; but it is probably a safe one.

Then we are on the main Albert road again, and after some rapid miles I find myself kindly welcomed by one of the most famous leaders of the war. There, in a small room, which has surely seen work of the first importance to our victories on the Somme, a great General discusses the situation and the future with that same sober and reasoned confidence I have found everywhere among the representatives of our Higher Command. "Are we approaching victory? Yes; but it is too soon to use the great word itself. Everything is going well; but the enemy is still very strong. This year will decide it; but may not end it."

* * * * *

So far my recollections of March 3rd. But this is now April 26th, and all the time that I have been writing these recollections, thought has been leaping forward to the actual present—to the huge struggle now pending between Arras and Rheims—to the news that comes crowding in, day by day, of the American preparations in aid of the Allies—to all that is at stake for us and for you. Your eyes are now turned like ours to the battle-line in France. You triumph—and you suffer—with us!

No. 6

May 3rd, 1917.

DEAR MR. ROOSEVELT,—My last letter left me returning to our village lodgings under the wing of G.H.Q. after a memorable day on the Somme battle-fields. That night the talk at the Visitors' Château, during and after a very simple dinner in an old panelled room, was particularly interesting and animated. The morning's newspapers had just arrived from England, with the official communiques of the morning. We were pushing nearer and nearer to Bapaume; in the fighting of the preceding day we had taken another 128 prisoners; and the King had sent his congratulations to Sir Douglas Haig and the Army on the German withdrawal under "the steady and persistent pressure" of the British Army "from carefully prepared and strongly fortified positions—a fitting sequel to the fine achievements of my Army last year in the Battle of the Somme." There was also a report on the air-fighting and air-losses of February—to which I will return.

It was, of course, already obvious that the German retreat on the Somme was not—so far—going to yield us any very large captures of men or guns. Prisoners were indeed collected every day, but there were no "hauls" such as, little more than a month after this evening of March 3rd, were to mark the very different course of the Battle of Arras. Discussion turned upon the pace of the German retreat and the possible rate of our pursuit. "Don't forget," said an officer, "that they are moving over good ground, while the pursuit has to move over bad ground—roads with craters in them, ground so pitted with shell-holes that you can scarcely drive a peg between them, demolished bridges, villages that give scarcely any cover, and so on. The enemy has his guns with him; ours have to be pushed up over the bad ground. His machine-guns are always in picked and prepared positions; ours have to be improvised."

And also—"Don't forget the weather!" said another. Every misty day—and there were many in February—was very skilfully turned to account. Whenever the weather conditions made it impossible to use the eyes of our Air Service, men would say to each other on our side, "He'll go back a lot to-day!—somewhere or other." But in spite of secrecy and fog, how little respite we had given him! The enemy losses in casualties, prisoners, and stores during February were certainly considerable; not to speak of the major loss of all, that of the strongly fortified line on which two years of the most arduous and ingenious labour that even Germany can give had been lavished. "And almost everywhere," writes an eye-witness, "he was hustled and harried much more than is generally known." As you go eastward, for instance, across the evacuated ground you notice everywhere signs of increasing haste and flurry, such as the less complete felling of trees and telegraph posts. It was really a fine performance for our infantry and our cavalry patrols, necessarily unsupported by *anything like our full artillery strength,* to keep up the constant pressure they did on an enemy who enjoyed almost the full protection of his. It was dreadful country to live and fight in after the Germans had gone back over it, much worse than anything that troops have to face after any ordinary capture of an enemy line.

The fact is that old axioms are being everywhere revised in the light of this war. In former wars the extreme difficulty of a retreat in the face of the enemy was taken for granted. But this war—I am trying to summarise some first-hand opinion as it has reached me—has modified this point of view considerably.

We know now that for any serious attack on an enemy who has plenty of machine-guns and plenty of successive well-wired positions a great mass of heavy and other artillery is absolutely indispensable. And over ground deliberately wrecked and obstructed such artillery *must* take time to bring up. And yet—to repeat—how rapidly, how "persistently" all difficulties considered, to use the King's adjective, has the British Army pressed on the heels of the retreating enemy!

None of the officers with whom I talked believed that anything more could have been done by us than was done. "If it had been we who were retreating," writes one of them, "and the Germans who were pursuing, I do not believe they would have pushed us so hard or caused us as much loss, for all their pride in their staff work."

And it is, of course, evident from what has happened since I parted from my hosts at the Château, that we have now amply succeeded during the last few weeks in bringing the retreating enemy to bay. No more masked withdrawals, no more skilful evasions, for either Hindenburg or his armies! The victories of Easter week on and beyond the Vimy Ridge, and the renewed British attack of the last few days—I am writing on May 1st—together with the magnificent French advance towards Laon and to the east of Reims, have been so many fresh and crushing testimonies to the vitality and gathering force of the Allied armies.

What is to be the issue we wait to see. But at least, after the winter lull, it is once more joined; and with such an army as the War Office and the nation together, during these three years, have fashioned to his hand—so trained, so equipped, so fired with a common and inflexible spirit—Sir Douglas Haig and his lieutenants will not fail the hopes of Great Britain, of France—and of America!

At the beginning of March these last words could not have been added. There was an American professor not far from me at dinner, and we discussed the "blazing indiscretion" of Herr Zimmermann's Mexican letter. But he knew no more than I. Only I remember with pleasure the general tone of all the conversation about America that I either engaged in or listened to at Headquarters just a month before the historic meeting of Congress. It was one of intelligent sympathy with the difficulties in your way, coupled with a quiet confidence that the call of civilisation and humanity would very soon—and irrevocably—decide the attitude of America towards the war.

* * * * *

The evening at the Château passed only too quickly, and we were sad to say good-bye, though it left me still the prospect of further conversation with some members of the Intelligence Staff on my return journey from Paris and those points of the French line for which, thanks to the courtesy of the French Headquarters, I was now bound.

The last night under the little schoolmistress's quiet roof amid the deep stillness of the village was a wakeful one for me. The presence of the New Armies, as of some vast, impersonal, and yet intensely living thing, seemed to be all around me. First, as an organisation, as the amazing product of English patriotic intelligence devoted to one sole end—the defence of civilisation against the immoral attack of the strongest military machine in the world. And then, so to speak, as a moral entity, for my mind was full of the sights and sounds of the preceding days, and the Army appeared to me, not only as the mighty instrument for war which it already is, but as a training school for the Empire, likely to have incalculable effect upon the future.

How much I have heard of *training* since my arrival in France! It is not a word that has been so far representative of our English temper. Far from it. The central idea of English life and politics, said Mr. Bright, "is the assertion of personal liberty." It was, I suppose, this assertion of personal liberty which drove our extreme Liberal wing before the war into that determined fighting of the Naval and Military Estimates year after year, that determined hatred of anything that looked like "militarism," and that constant belittlement of the soldier and his profession which so nearly handed us over, for lack of a reasonable "militarism," to the tender mercies of the German variety.

But, years ago, Matthew Arnold dared to say, in face of the general British approval of Mr. Bright, that there is, after all, something greater than the "assertion of personal liberty," than the freedom to "do as you like"; and he put forward against it the notion of "the nation in its collected and corporate character" controlling the individual will in the name of an interest wider than that of individuals.

What he had in view was surely just what we are witnessing in Great Britain to-day—what we are about to witness in your own country—a nation becoming the voluntary servant of an idea, and for that idea submitting itself to forms of life quite new to it, and far removed from all its ordinary habits; giving up the freedom to do as it likes; accepting the extremities of discomfort, hardship, and pain—death itself—rather than abandon the idea; and so putting itself to school, resolutely and of its own free will, that when its piece of self-imposed education is done, it can no more be the same as it was before than the youth who has yielded himself loyally to the pounding and stretching of any strenuous discipline, intellectual or physical.

Training—"askêsis"—with either death, or the loss of all that makes honourable life, as the ultimate sanction behind the process, that is the present preoccupation of this nation in arms. Even the football games I saw going on in the course of our drive to Albert were all part of this training. They are no mere amusement, though they are amusement. They are part of the system by which men are persuaded—not driven—to submit themselves to a scheme of careful physical training, even in their times of rest; by which they find themselves so invigorated that they end by demanding it.

As for the elaboration of everything else in this frightful art of war, the ever-multiplying staff courses, the bombing and bayonet schools, the special musketry and gas schools, the daily and weekly development of aviation, the technical industry and skill, both among the gunners abroad and the factory workers at home, which has now made our artillery the terror of the German army: a woman can only realise it with a shudder, and find comfort in two beliefs. First, that the whole horrible process of war has *not* brutalised the British soldier—you remember the Army Commander whom I quoted in an earlier letter!—that he still remains human and warm-hearted through it all, protected morally by the ideal he willingly serves. Secondly, in the conviction that this relentless struggle is the only means that remains to us of so chaining up the wild beast of war, as the Germans have let it loose upon the world, that our children and grandchildren at least shall live in peace, and have time given them to work out a more reasonable scheme of things.

But, at any rate; we have gone a long way from the time when Matthew Arnold, talking with "the manager of the Claycross works in Derbyshire" during the Crimean War, "when our want of soldiers was much felt and some people were talking of conscription," was told by his companion that "sooner than submit to conscription the population of that district would flee to the mines, and lead a sort of Robin Hood life underground." An illuminating passage, in more ways than one, by the way, as contrasted with the present state of things!—since it both shows the stubbornness of the British temper in defence of "doing as it likes," when no spark of an ideal motive fires it; and also brings out its equal

43

stubbornness to-day in support of a cause which it feels to be supreme over the individual interest and will.

But the stubbornness, the discipline, the sacrifice of the armies in the field are not all we want. The stubbornness of the nation *at home*, of the men and the women, is no less necessary to the great end. In these early days of March every week's news was bringing home to England the growing peril of the submarine attack. Would the married women, the elder women of the nation, rise to the demand for personal thought and saving, for *training*—in the matter of food— with the same eager goodwill as thousands of the younger women had shown in meeting the armies' demand for munitions? For the women heads of households have it largely in their hands.

The answer at the beginning of March was matter for anxiety. It is still matter for anxiety now—at the beginning of May.

Let us, however, return for a little to the Army. What would the marvellous organisation which England has produced in three years avail us, without the spirit in it,—the body, without the soul? All through these days I have been conscious, in the responsible men I have been meeting, of ideals of which no one talks, except when, on very rare occasions, it happens to be in the day's work like anything else to talk of ideals—but which are, in fact, omnipresent.

I find, for instance, among my War Office Notes, a short address given in the ordinary course of duty by an unnamed commandant to his officer-cadets. It appears here, in its natural place, just as part of the whole; revealing for a moment the thoughts which constantly underlie it.

"Believe me when I tell you that I have never found an officer who worked who did not come through. Only ill-health and death stand in your way. The former you can guard against in a great measure. The latter comes to us all, and for a soldier, a soldier's death is the finest of all. Fear of death does not exist for the man who has led a good and honest life. You must discipline your bodies and your minds—your bodies by keeping them healthy and strong, your minds by prayer and thought."

As to the relation between officers and men, that also is not talked about much, except in its more practical and workaday aspects—the interest taken by officers in the men's comfort and welfare, their readiness to share in the men's games and amusements, and so on. And no one pretends that the whole British Army is an army of "plaster saints," that every officer is the "little father" of his men, and all relations ideal.

But what becomes evident, as one penetrates a little nearer to the great organism, is a sense of passionate responsibility in all the finer minds of the Army towards their men, a readiness to make any sacrifice for them, a deep and abiding sense of their sufferings and dangers, of all that they are giving to their country. How this comes out again and again in the innumerable death-stories of British officers—those few words that commemorate them in the daily newspapers! And how evident is the profound response of the men to such a temper in their officers! There is not a day's action in the field—I am but quoting the eye-witnesses—that does not bring out such facts. Let a senior

44

officer—an "old and tried soldier"—speak. He is describing a walk over a battlefield on the Ancre after one of our victories there last November:

"It is a curious thing to walk over enemy trenches that I have watched like a tiger for weeks and weeks. But what of the boys who took those trenches, with their eleven rows of barbed wire in front of them? I don't think I ever before to-day rated the British soldier at his proper value. His sufferings in this weather are indescribable. When he is not in the trenches his discomforts are enough to kill any ordinary mortal. When he is in the trenches it is a mixture between the North Pole and Hell. And yet when the moment comes he jumps up and charges at the impossible—and conquers it! ... Some of the poor fellows who lay there as they fell looked to me absolutely noble, and I thought of their families who were aching for news of them and hoping against hope that they would not be left unburied in their misery.

"All the loving and tender thoughts that are lavished on them are not enough. There are no words to describe the large hearts of these men. God bless 'em! And what of the French on whose soil they lie? Can they ever forget the blood that is mingled with their own? I hope not. I don't think England has ever had as much cause to be proud as she has to-day."

Ah! such thoughts and feelings cut deep. They would be unbearable but for the saving salt of humour in which this whole great gathering of men, so to speak, moves suspended, as though in an atmosphere. It is everywhere. Coarse or refined, it is the universal protection, whether from the minor discomforts or the more frightful risks of war. Volumes could be filled, have already been filled, with it—volumes to which your American soldier when he gets to France in his thousands will add considerably—pages all his own! I take this touch in passing from a recent letter:

"A sergeant in my company [writes a young officer] was the other day buried by a shell. He was dug out with difficulty. As he lay, not seriously injured, but sputtering and choking, against the wall of the trench, his C.O. came by. 'Well, So-and-so, awfully sorry! Can I do anything for you?' 'Sir,' said the sergeant with dignity, still struggling out of the mud, '*I want a separate peace!*'"

And here is another incident that has just come across me. Whether it is Humour or Pathos I do not know. In this scene they are pretty close together— the great Sisters!

A young flying officer, in a night attack, was hit by a shrapnel bullet from below. He thought it had struck his leg, but was so absorbed in dropping his bombs and bringing down his machine safely that, although he was aware of a feeling of faintness, he thought no more of it till he had landed in the aerodrome. Then it was discovered that his leg had been shot away, was literally hanging by a shred of skin, and how he had escaped bleeding to death nobody could quite understand. As it was, he had dropped his bombs, and he insisted on making his report in hospital.

He recovered from the subsequent operation, and in hospital, some weeks afterwards, his C.O. appeared, with the news of his recommendation for the D.S.O. The boy, for he was little more, listened with eyes of amused incredulity, opening wider and wider as the Colonel proceeded. When the communication was over, and the C.O., attributing the young man's silence to weakness or grateful emotion, had passed on, the nurse beside the bed saw the patient bury his head in the pillow with a queer sound of exasperation, and caught the words, "I call it *perfectly childish!*"

That an act so simple, so all in the bargain, should have earned the D.S.O. seemed in the eyes of the doer to degrade the honour!

* * * * *

With this true tale I have come back to a recollection of the words of the flying officer in charge of the aerodrome mentioned in my second letter, after he had described to me the incessant raiding and fighting of our airmen behind the enemy lines.

"Many of them don't come back. What then? *They will have done their job.*"

The report which reaches the château on our last evening illustrates this casual remark. It shows that 89 machines were lost during February, 60 of them German. We claimed 41 of these, and 23 British machines were "missing" or "brought down."

But as I write the concluding words of this letter (May 3rd) a far more startling report—that for April—lies before me. "There has not been a month of such fighting since the war began, and the losses have never reached such a tremendous figure," says the *Times*. The record number so far was that for September 1916, in the height of the Somme fighting—322. But during April, according to the official reports, "the enormous number of 717 aeroplanes were brought to earth as the result of air-fights or by gun-fire." Of these, 369 were German—269 of them brought down by the British and 98 by the French. The British lost 147; the French and Belgian, if the German claims can be trusted, 201.

It is a terrible list, and a terrible testimony to the extreme importance and intensity of the air-fighting now going on. How few of us, except those who have relatives or dear friends in the air-service, realise at all the conditions of this fighting—its daring, its epic range, its constant development!

All the men in it are young. None of them can have such a thing as a nerve. Anyone who betrays the faintest suspicion of one in his first flights is courteously but firmly returned to his regiment. In peace the airman sees this solid earth of ours as no one else sees it; and in war he makes acquaintance by day and night with all its new and strange aspects, amid every circumstance of danger and excitement, with death always at hand, his life staked, not only against the enemy and all his devices on land and above it, but against wind and cloud, against the treacheries of the very air itself.

In the midst of these conditions the fighting airman shoots, dodges, pursues, and dives, intent only on one thing, the destruction of his enemy, while the observer photographs, marks his map with every gun-emplacement, railway station, dump of food or ammunition, unconcerned by the flying shells or the strange dives and swoops of the machine.

But apart from active fighting, take such a common experience as what is called "a long reconnaissance." Pilot and observer receive their orders to reconnoitre "thoroughly" a certain area. It may be winter, and the cold at the height of many thousand feet may be formidable indeed. No matter. The thing is done, and, after hours in the freezing air, the machine makes for home; through a winter evening, perhaps, as we saw the two splendid biplanes, near the northern section of the line, sailing far above our heads into the sunset, that first day of our journey. The reconnaissance is over, and here is the first-hand testimony of one who has taken part in many, as to what it means in endurance and fatigue:

"Both pilot and observer are stiff with the cold. In winter it is often necessary to help them out of the machine and attend to the chilled parts of the body to avoid frost-bite. Their faces are drawn with the continual strain. They are deaf from the roar of the engine. Their eyes are bloodshot, and their whole bodies are racked with every imaginable ache. For the next few hours they are good for nothing but rest, though sleep is generally hard to get. But before turning in the observer must make his report and hand it in to the proper quarter."

So much for the nights which are rather for observation than fighting, though fighting constantly attends them. But the set battles in the air, squadron with squadron, man with man, the bombers in the centre, the fighting machines surrounding and protecting them, are becoming more wonderful, more daring, more complicated every month. "You'll see"—I recall once more the words of our Flight-Commander, spoken amid the noise and movement of a score of practising machines, five weeks before the battle of Arras—"when the great move begins *we shall get the mastery again, as we did on the Somme.*"

Ask the gunners in the batteries of the April advance, as they work below the signalling planes; ask the infantry whom the gunners so marvellously protect, as to the truth of the prophecy!

"Our casualties are *really* light," writes an officer in reference to some of the hot fighting of the past month. Thanks, apparently, to the ever-growing precision of our artillery methods; which again depend on aeroplane and balloon information. So it is that the flying forms in the upper air become for the soldier below so many symbols of help and protection. He is restless when they are not there. And let us remember that aeroplanes were first used for artillery observation, not three years ago, in the battle of Aisne, after the victory of the Marne.

But the night in the quiet village wears away. To-morrow we shall be flying through the pleasant land of France, bound for Paris and Lorraine. For I am turning now to a new task. On our own line I have been trying to describe, for those who care to listen, the crowding impressions left on a woman-witness by the huge development in the last twelve months of the British military effort in France. But now, as I go forward into this beautiful country, which I have loved next to my own all my life, there are new purposes in my mind, and three memorable words in my ears:

"*Reparation—Restitution—Guarantees!*"

47

No. 7

May 10th, 1917.

DEAR MR. ROOSEVELT,—We are then, for a time, to put France, and not the British line, in the forefront of these later letters. For when I went out on this task, as I think you know, I had two objects in mind—intimately connected. The first was to carry on that general story of the British effort, which I began last year under your inspiration, down to the opening of this year's campaign. And the second was to try and make more people in this country, and more people in America, realise—as acutely and poignantly as I could—what it is we are really fighting for; what is the character of the enemy we are up against; what are the sufferings, outrages, and devastations which have been inflicted on France, in particular, by the wanton cruelty and ambition of Germany; for which she herself must be made to suffer and pay, if civilisation and freedom are to endure.

With this second intention, I was to have combined, by the courtesy of the French Headquarters, a visit to certain central portions of the French line, including Soissons, Reims, and Verdun. But by the time I reached France the great operations that have since marked the Soissons-Reims front were in active preparation; roads and motor-cars were absorbed by the movements of troops and stores; Reims and Verdun were under renewed bombardment; and visits to this section of the French line were entirely held up. The French authorities, understanding that I chiefly wished to see for myself some of the wrecked and ruined villages and towns dealt with in the French official reports, suggested, first Senlis and the battle-fields of the Ourcq, and then Nancy, the ruined villages of Lorraine, and that portion of their eastern frontier line where, simultaneously with the Battle of the Marne, General Castelnau directed from the plateau of Amance and the Grand Couronné that strong defence of Nancy which protected—and still protects—the French right, and has baulked all the German attempts to turn it.

Meanwhile, in the early days of March, the German retreat, south of the Somme and in front of the French line, was not yet verified; and the worst devastation of the war—the most wanton crime, perhaps, that Germany has so far committed—was not yet accomplished. I had left France before it was fully known, and could only realise, by hot sympathy from a distance, the passionate thrill of fury and wild grief which swept through France when the news began to come in from the evacuated districts. British correspondents with the advancing armies of the Allies have seen deeds of barbarism which British eyes and hearts will never forget, and have sent the news of them through the world. The destruction of Coucy and Ham, the ruin and plunder of the villages, the shameless loot everywhere, the hideous ill-treatment of the country folk, the deportation of boys and girls, the massacre of the fruit trees—these things have gone deep into the very soul of France, burning away—except in the minds of a few incorrigible fanatics—whatever foolish "pacificism" was there, and steeling the mind and will of the nation afresh to that victory which can alone bring expiation, punishment, and a peace worth the name. But, everywhere, the ruins with which northern, central, and eastern France are covered, whether they were caused by the ordinary processes of war or not, are equally part of the guilt of

Germany. In the country which I saw last year on the Belgian border, from the great phantom of Ypres down to Festubert, the ravage is mainly the ravage of war. Incessant bombardment from the fighting lines has crumbled village after village into dust, or gashed the small historic towns and the stately country houses. There is no deliberate use of torch and petrol, as in the towns farther south and east. Ypres, however, was deliberately shelled into fragments day after day; and Arras is only a degree less carefully ruined. And whatever the military pretext may be, the root question remains—"Why are the Germans *in France at all*?" What brought them there but their own determination, in the words of the Secret Report of 1913 printed in the French Yellow book, to "strengthen and extend *Deutschtum* (Germanism) throughout the entire world"? Every injury that poor France in self-defence, or the Allies at her side, are forced to inflict on the villages and towns which express and are interwoven with the history and genius of the French, is really a German crime. There is no forgiveness for what Germany has done—none! She has tried to murder a people; and but for the splendid gifts of that people, she would have achieved her end.

Perhaps the tragedy of what is to be seen and heard at Senlis, on the battle-grounds of the Ourcq, and in the villages of Lorraine, was heightened for me by the beauty of the long drive south from the neighbourhood of G.H.Q.—some hundred and forty miles. It was a cold but clear March day. We had but parted from snow a little while, and we were soon to find it again. But on this day, austerely bright, the land of France unrolled before us its long succession of valley and upland, upland and valley. Here, no trace of the invader; generally speaking no signs of the armies; for our route lay, on an average, some forty miles behind the line. All was peace, solitude even; for the few women, old men, and boys on the land scarcely told in the landscape. But every mile was rich in the signs and suggestion of an old and most human civilisation—farms, villages, towns, the carefully tended woods, the fine roads running their straight unimpeded course over hill and dale, bearing witness to a *State sense,* of which we possess too little in this country.

We stopped several times on the journey—I remember a puncture, involving a couple of hours' delay, somewhere north of Beauvais—and found ourselves talking in small hot rooms with peasant families of all ages and stages, from the blind old grandmother, like a brooding Fate in the background, to the last toddling baby. How friendly they were, in their own self-respecting way!—the grave-faced elder women, the young wives, the children. The strength of the *family* in France seems to me still overwhelming—would we had more of it left in England! The prevailing effect was of women everywhere *carrying on*—making no parade of it, being indeed accustomed to work, and familiar with every detail of the land; having merely added the tasks of their husbands and sons to their own, and asking no praise for it. The dignity, the essential refinement and intelligence—for all their homely speech—of these solidly built, strong-faced women, in the central districts of France, is still what it was when George Sand drew her Berri peasants, nearly a hundred years ago.

49

Then darkness fell, and in the darkness we went through an old, old town where are the French General Headquarters. Sentries challenged us to right and left, and sent us forward again with friendly looks. The day had been very long, and presently, as we approached Paris, I fell asleep in my corner, only to be roused with a start by a glare of lights, and more sentries. The *barrière* of Paris!—shining out into the night.

Two days in Paris followed; every hour crowded with talk, and the vivid impressions of a moment when, from beyond Compiègne and Soissons—some sixty miles from the Boulevards—the French airmen flying over the German lines were now bringing back news every morning and night of fresh withdrawals, fresh villages burning, as the sullen enemy relaxed his hold.

On the third day, a most courteous and able official of the French Foreign Office took us in charge, and we set out for Senlis on a morning chill and wintry indeed, but giving little sign of the storm it held in leash.

To reach Senlis one must cross the military *enceinte* of Paris. Many visitors from Paris and other parts of France, from England, or from America, have seen by now the wreck of its principal street, and have talked with the Abbé Dourlent, the "Archiprêtre" of the cathedral, whose story often told has lost but little of its first vigour and simplicity, to judge at least by its effect on two of his latest visitors.

We took the great northern road out of Paris, which passes scenes memorable in the war of 1870. On both sides of us, at frequent intervals, across the flat country, were long lines of trenches, and belts of barbed wire, most of them additions to the defences of Paris since the Battle of the Marne. It is well to make assurance doubly sure! But although, as we entered the Forest of Chantilly, the German line was no more than some thirty-odd miles away, and since the Battle of the Aisne, two and a half years ago, it has run, practically, as it still ran in the early days of this last March, the notion of any fresh attack on Paris seemed the merest dream. It was indeed a striking testimony to the power of the modern defensive—this absolute security in which Paris and its neighbourhood has lived and moved all that time, with—up to a few weeks ago—the German batteries no farther off than the suburbs of Soissons. How good to remember, as one writes, all that has happened since I was in Senlis!— and the increased distance that now divides the German hosts from the great prize on which they had set their hearts.

How fiercely they had set their hearts on it, the old Curé of Senlis, who is the chief depository of the story of the town, was to make us feel anew.

One enters Senlis from Paris by the main street, the Rue de la République, which the Germans deliberately and ruthlessly burnt on September 2nd and 3rd, 1914. We moved slowly along it through the blackened ruins of houses large and small, systematically fired by the German *pétroleurs*, in revenge for a supposed attack by civilians upon the entering German troops. *Les civils ont tiré*—it is the universal excuse for these deeds of wanton barbarism, and for the hideous cruelties to men, women, and children that have attended them— beginning with that incident which first revealed to a startled world the true character of the men directing the German Army—the burning and sack of Louvain. It is to be hoped that renewed and careful investigation will be made—(much preliminary inquiry has already of course taken place)—after the war into all these cases. My own impression from what I have heard, seen, and read—for what it may be worth—is that the plea is almost invariably false; but that the state of panic and excitement into which the German temperament falls, with extraordinary readiness, under the strain of battle, together with the drunkenness of troops traversing a rich wine-growing country, have often accounted for an honest, but quite mistaken belief in the minds of German soldiers, without excusing at all the deeds to which it led. Of this abnormal excitability, the old Curé of Senlis gave one or two instances which struck me.

We came across him by chance in the cathedral—the beautiful cathedral I have heard Walter Pater describe, in my young Oxford days, as one of the loveliest and gracefullest things in French Gothic. Fortunately, though the slender belfry and the roof were repeatedly struck by shrapnel in the short bombardment of the town, no serious damage was done. We wandered round the church alone, delighting our eyes with the warm golden white of the stone, the height of the grooved arches, the flaming fragments of old glass, when we saw the figure of an old priest come slowly down the aisle, his arms folded. He looked at us rather dreamily and passed. Our guide, Monsieur P., followed and spoke to him. "Monsieur, you are the Abbé Dourlent?"

"I am, sir. What can I do for you?"

Something was said about English ladies, and the Curé courteously turned back. "Will the ladies come into the Presbytère?" We followed him across the small cathedral square to the old house in which he lived, and were shown into a bare dining-room, with a table, some chairs, and a few old religious engravings on the walls. He offered us chairs and sat down himself.

"You would like to hear the story of the German occupation?" He thought a little before beginning, and I was struck with his strong, tired face, the powerful mouth and jaw, and above them, eyes which seemed to have lost the power of smiling, though I guessed them to be naturally full of a pleasant shrewdness, of what the French call *malice*, which is not the English "malice." He was rather difficult to follow here and there, but from his spoken words and from a written account he placed in my hands, I put together the following story:

"It was August 30th, 1914, when the British General Staff arrived in Senlis. That same evening, they left it for Dammartin. All day, and the next two days, French and English troops passed through the town. What was happening? Would there be no fighting in defence of Paris—only thirty miles away? Wednesday, September 2nd—that was the day the guns began, our guns and theirs, to the north of Senlis. But, in the course of that day, we knew finally there would be no battle between us and Paris. The French troops were going—the English were going. They left us—marching eastward. Our hearts were very sore as we saw them go.

"Two o'clock on Wednesday—the first shell struck the cathedral. I had just been to the top of the belfry to see, if I could, from what direction the enemy was coming. The bombardment lasted an hour and a half. At four o'clock they entered. If you had seen them!"

The old Curé raised himself on his seat, trying to imitate the insolent bearing of the German cavalry as they led the way through the old town which they imagined would be the last stage on their way to Paris.

"They came in, shouting '*Paris—Nach Paris!*' maddened with excitement. They were all singing—they were like men beside themselves."

"What did they sing, Monsieur le Curé?—Deutschland über alles'?"

"Oh, no, madame, not at all. They sang hymns. It was an extraordinary sight. They seemed possessed. They were certain that in a few hours they would be in Paris. They passed through the town, and then, just south of the town, they stopped. Our people show the place. It was the nearest they ever got to Paris.

"Presently, an officer, with an escort, a general apparently, rode through the town, pulled up at the Hôtel de Ville, and asked for the Maire—angrily, like a man in a passion. But the Maire—M. Odent—was there, waiting, on the steps of the Hôtel de Ville.

"Monsieur Odent was my friend—he gave me his confidence. He had resisted his nomination as Mayor as long as he could, and accepted it only as an imperative duty. He was an employer, whom his workmen loved. One of them used to say—'When one gets into M. Odent's employ, one lives and dies there.' Just before the invasion, he took his family away. Then he came back, with the presentiment of disaster. He said to me—'I persuaded my wife to go. It was hard. We are much attached to each other—but now I am free, ready for all that may come.'

"Well, the German general said to him roughly:

"'Is your town quiet? Can we circulate safely?'

"M. Odent said, 'Yes. There is no quieter town in France than Senlis.'

"'Are there still any soldiers here?'

"M. Odent had seen the French troops defiling through the town all the morning. The bombardment had made it impossible to go about the streets. As far as he knew there were none left. He answered, 'No.'

"He was taken off, practically under arrest, to the Hôtel, and told to order a dinner for thirty, with ice and champagne. Then his secretary joined him and proposed that the *adjoints*, or Mayor's assistants, should be sent for.

"'No,' said M. Odent, 'one victim is enough.' You see he foresaw everything. We all knew what had happened in Belgium and the Ardennes.

"The German officer questioned him again.

"'Why have your people gone?—why are these houses, these shops, shut? There must be lights *everywhere*—all through the night!'

"Suddenly—shots!—in the Rue de la République. In a few seconds there was a furious fusillade, accompanied by the rattle of machine guns. The officer sprang up.

"'So this is your quiet town, Monsieur le Maire! I arrest you, and you shall answer with your life for the lives of my soldiers.'

"Two men with revolvers were set to guard him. The officer himself presently took him outside the town, and left him under guard, at the little village of Poteau, at the edge of a wood."

* * * * *

What had happened? Unluckily for Senlis and M. Odent, some of the French rear-guard—infantry stragglers, and a small party of Senegalese troops—were still in the southern quarter of the town when the Germans entered. They opened fire from a barrack near the Paris entrance and a sharp engagement followed which lasted several hours, with casualties on both sides. The Germans got the better, and were then free to wreak their fury on the town.

They broke into the houses, plundered the wine shops, first of all, and took fifty hostages, of whom twenty-six perished. And at half-past five, while the fighting was still going on, the punitive burning of the town began, by a cyclist section told off for the work and furnished with every means for doing it effectively. These men, according to an eyewitness, did their work with wild shouts—"*cris sauvages.*"

A hundred and seventeen houses were soon burning fiercely. On that hot September evening, the air was like a furnace. Before long the streets were full of blazing débris. Two persons who had hidden themselves in their cellars died of suffocation; yet to appear in the streets was to risk death at the hands of some drunk or maddened soldier.

At the opening of the French attack, a German officer rushed to the hospital, which was full of wounded, in search of francs-tireurs. Arrived there, he saw an old man, a chronic patient of the hospital and half idiotic, standing on the steps of the building. He blew the old man's brains out. He then forced his way into the hospital, pointing his revolver at the French wounded, who thought their last hour had come. He himself was wounded, and at last appeared to yield to the remonstrances of the Sister in charge, and allowed his wound to be dressed. But in the middle of the dressing, he broke away without his tunic, and helmetless, in a state of mad excitement, and presently reappeared with a file of soldiers. Placing them in the street opposite the rooms occupied by the French wounded, he ordered them to fire a volley. No one was hurt, though several beds were struck. Then the women's wards were searched. Two sick men, *éclopés* without visible wounds, were dragged out of their beds and would have been bayoneted then and there but for the entreaties of the nurses, who ultimately released them.

An awful night followed in the still burning or smouldering town. Meanwhile, at nine o'clock in the evening a party of German officers betook themselves to the hamlet of Poteau—a village north of Senlis—where M. Odent had been kept under guard since the afternoon. Six other hostages were produced, and they were all marched off to a field near Chamant at the edge of a wood. Here the Maire was called up and interrogated. His companion, eight or nine metres away, too far to hear what was said, watched the scene. As I think of it, I seem to see in the southern sky the glare of burning Senlis; above it, and spread over the stubble fields in which the party stood, a peaceful moonlight. In his written account, the Curé specially mentions the brightness of the harvest moon.

Presently the Maire came back to the six, and said to one, Benoit Decreys, "Adieu, my poor Benoit, we shall not see each other again —they are going to shoot me." He took his crucifix, his purse containing a sum of money, and some papers, out of his pocket, and asked that they should be given to his family. Then pressing the hands held out to him, he said good-bye to them all, and went back with a firm step to the group of officers. Two soldiers were called up, and the Maire was placed at ten paces' distance. The soldiers fired, and M. Odent fell without a sound. He was hastily buried under barely a foot of earth, and his six companions were left on the spot through the night expecting the same fate, till the morning, when they were released. Five other hostages, "gathered haphazard in the streets," were shot the same night in the neighbourhood of Chamant.

Meanwhile the Curé, knowing nothing of what was happening to the Maire, had been thinking for his parishioners and his church. When the bombardment began he gathered together about a hundred and twenty of them, who had apparently no cellars to take refuge in, and after sheltering them in the Presbytère for a time, he sent them with one of his *vicaires* out of the town. Then—to continue his narrative:

"I went to the southern portal of the cathedral, and stood there trembling at every burst of shrapnel that struck the belfry and the roof, and running out into the open, at each pause, to be sure that the church was still there. When the firing ceased, I went back to the Presbytère.

"Presently, furious sounds of blows from the *place*. I went out. I saw some enemy cyclists, armed with fragments of stone, breaking in one of the cathedral doors, another, with a hatchet, attacking the belfry door. At the sight of me, they rushed at me with their revolvers, demanding that I should take them to the top of the belfry. 'You have a machine gun there!' 'Nothing of the sort, monsieur. See for yourselves.' I unlocked the door, and just as I put my foot on the first step, the fusillade in the town began. The soldiers started. 'You are our prisoner!' cried their chief, turning to me, as though to seize me.

"'I know it. You have me in your hands.' I went up before them, as quickly as my age allowed. They searched everywhere, and, of course, found nothing. They ran down and disappeared."

But that was not the end of the Abbé's trouble. He was presently sent for to the German Headquarters, at the Hotel du Grand Cerf, where the table spread for thirty people, by the order of M. Odent, was still waiting for its guests. The conversation here between the Curé and the officer of high rank who spoke to him is worth repeating. From the tenor of it, the presumption is that the officer was a Catholic—probably a Bavarian.

"I asked leave to go back to the Presbytère.

"'Better stay here, Monsieur le Curé. You will be safer. The burning is going on. To-morrow, your town will be only a heap of ruins.'

"'What is our crime?'

"'Listen to that fusillade. Your inhabitants are attacking us, as they did at Louvain. Louvain has ceased to exist! We will make of Senlis another Louvain,

54

so that Paris and France may know how we treat those who may imitate you. We have found small shot (*chevrotines*) in the body of one of our officers.'

"'Already?'—I thought. How had there been any time for the post-mortem? But I was too crushed to speak.

"'And also from your belfry we have been fired on!'

"At that I recovered myself.

"'Sir—what may have passed in the streets, I cannot say. But as to the cathedral I formally deny your charge. Since war broke out, I have always had the keys of the belfry. I did not even give them to your soldiers, who made me take them there. Do you wish me to swear it?'

"The officer looked at me.

"'No need. You are a Catholic priest. I see you are sincere.'

"I bowed."

A scene that throws much light! A false charge—an excited reference to Louvain—monstrous threat—the temper, that is, of panic, which is the mother of cruelty. At that very moment, the German troops in the Rue de la Republique were driving parties of French civilians in front of them, as a protection from the Senegalese troops who were still firing from houses near the Paris exit from the town. Four or five of these poor people were killed by French bullets; a child of five forced along, with her mother, was shot in the thigh. Altogether some twenty or thirty civilians seem to have been killed.

Next day more houses were burnt. Then, for a time, the quiet of desolation. All the normal population were gone, or in the cellars. But twenty miles away to the southeast, great things were preparing. The German occupation of Senlis began, as we have seen, on a Wednesday, September 2nd. On Saturday the 5th, as we all know, the first shots were fired in that Battle of the Ourcq which was the western section of the Battle of the Marne. By that Saturday, already, writes the Abbé Dourlent:

"There was something changed in the attitude of the enemy. What had become of the brutal arrogance, the insolent cruelty of the first days? For three days and nights, the German troops, an army of 300,000 men, defiled through our streets. It was not the road to Paris, now, that they asked for—it was the way to Nanteuil, Ermenonville, the direction of the Marne. On the faces of the officers, one seemed to read disappointment and anxiety. Close to us, on the east, the guns were speaking, every day more fiercely. What was happening?"

All that the Curé knows is that in a house belonging to persons of his acquaintance, where some officers of the rear-guard left behind in Senlis are billeted, two of the young officers have been in tears—it is supposed, because of bad news. Another day, an armoured car rushes into Senlis from Paris; the men in it exchange some shots with the German soldiers in the principal *place*, and make off again, calling out, "Courage! Deliverance is coming!"

Then, on the 9th, just a week from the German entry, there is another fusillade in the streets. "It is the Zouaves, knocking at the doors, dragging out the conquerors of yesterday, now a humbled remnant, with their hands in the air."

And the Curé goes on to compare Senlis to the sand which the Creator showed to the sea. "Thus far shalt thou go, and no farther." "The grain of sand is Senlis, still red with the flames which have devoured her, and with the blood of her victims. To these barbarians she cries—'You want Paris?—you want France? Halt! No road through here!'"

* * * * *

This combination of the Curé's written and spoken account is as close to the facts as I can make it. His narrative as he gave it to me, of what he had seen and felt, was essentially simple, and, to judge from the French official reports, with which I have compared it, essentially true. There are some discrepancies in detail, but nothing that matters. The murder of M. Odent, of the other hostages, of the civilians placed in front of the German troops, and of four or five other victims; the burning out by torch and explosive of half a flourishing town, because of a discreditable mistake, the fruit of panic and passion,—these crimes are indelibly marked on the record of Germany. She has done worse elsewhere. All the same, this too she will never efface. Let us imagine such things happening at Guildford, or Hatfield, or St. Albans!

We parted with M. le Curé just in time to meet a pleasant party of war correspondents at the very inn, the Hôtel du Cerf, which had been the German Headquarters during the occupation. The correspondents were on their way between the French Headquarters and the nearest points of the French line, Soissons or Compiègne, from whose neighbourhood every day the Germans were slowly falling back, and where the great attacks of the month of April were in active preparation. Then, after luncheon, we sallied out into the darkening afternoon, through the Forest of Ermenonville, and up to the great plateau, stretching north towards Soissons, southwards towards Meaux, and eastwards towards the Ourcq, where Maunoury's Sixth Army, striking from Paris and the west, and the English Army, striking from the south—aided by all the gallant French line from Château Thierry to the Grand Couronné—dealt that staggering blow against the German right which flung back the German host, and, weary as the way has been since, weary as it may still be, in truth, decided the war.

But the clouds hang lower as we emerge on the high bare plain. A few flakes—then, in a twinkling, a whirling snow-storm through which we can hardly see our way. But we fight through it, and along the roads every one of which is famous in the history of the battle. At our northernmost point we are about thirty miles from Soissons and the line. Columns of French infantry on the march, guns, ammunition, stores, field kitchens, pass us perpetually; the motor moves at a foot's pace, and we catch the young faces of the soldiers through the white thickened air. And our most animated and animating companion, Monsieur P——, with his wonderful knowledge of the battle, hails every landmark, identifies every farm and wood, even in what has become, in less than an hour, a white wilderness. But it is of one village only, of these many whose names are henceforth known to history, that I wish to speak—the village of Vareddes. In my next letter I propose to tell the ghastly story of the hostages of Vareddes.

No. 8

May 17th, 1917.

DEAR MR. ROOSEVELT,—Shall I ever forget that broad wintry plateau of the Ourcq, as it lay, at the opening of March, under its bed of snow, with its ruined villages, its graves scattered over the fields, its utter loneliness, save for the columns of marching soldiers in the roads, and the howling wind that rushed over the fields, the graves, the cemeteries, and whistled through the gaping walls of the poor churches and farms? This high spreading plain, which before the war was one scene of rural plenty and industrious peace, with its farm lands and orchards dropping gently from the forest country of Chantilly, Compiègne, and Ermenonville, down to the Ourcq and the Marne, will be a place of pilgrimage for generations to come. Most of the Battle of the Marne was fought on so vast a scale, over so wide a stretch of country—about 200 miles long, by 50 broad— that for the civilian spectator of the future it will never be possible to realise it as a whole, and very difficult even to realise any section of it, topographically, owing to the complication of the actions involved. But in the Battle of the Ourcq, the distances are comparatively small, the actions comparatively simple and intelligible, while all the circumstances of the particular struggle are so dramatic, and the stakes at issue so vast, that every incident is, as it were, writ large, and the memory absorbs them more easily.

An Englishwoman, too, may be glad it was in this conspicuous section of the battle-field, which will perhaps affect the imagination of posterity more easily than any other, that it fell to the British Army to play its part. To General Joffre the glory of the main strategic conception of the great retreat; to General Gallieni the undying honour of the rapid perception, the quick decision, which flung General Maunoury, with the 6th Army, on Von Kluck's flank and rear, at the first hint of the German general's swerve to the southeast; to General Maunoury himself, and his splendid troops, the credit of the battle proper, across the broad harvest fields of the Ourcq plateau. But the advance of the British troops from the south of the Marne, on the heels of Von Kluck, was in truth all-important to the success of Maunoury on the Ourcq. It was the British Expeditionary Force which made the hinge of the battle-line, and if that hinge had not been strong and supple—in all respects equal to its work—the sudden attack of the 6th Army, on the extreme left of the battle-line, and the victory of General Foch in the centre, might not have availed. In other words, had Von Kluck found the weak spot he believed in and struck for, all would have been different. But the weak spot existed only in the German imagination. The British troops whom Von Kluck supposed to be exhausted and demoralised, were in truth nothing of the sort. Rested and in excellent condition, they turned rejoicing upon the enemy, and, in concert with the French 6th Army, decided the German withdrawal. Every one of the six Armies aligned across France, from Paris to the Grand Couronne, had its own glorious task in the defeat of the German plans. But we were then so small a proportion of the whole, with our hundred and twenty thousand men, and we have become since so accustomed to count in millions, that perhaps our part in the "miracle of the Marne" is sometimes in danger of becoming a little blurred in the popular English—and American— conception of the battle. Is not the truth rather that we had a twofold share in it?

It was Von Kluck's miscalculation as to the English strength that tempted him to his eastward march; it was the quality of the British force and leadership, when Sir John French's opportunity came, that made the mistake a fatal one.

How different the aspect of the Ourcq plateau at the opening of the battle in 1914, from the snowy desolation under which we saw it! Perfect summer weather—the harvest stacks in the fields—a blazing sun by day, and a clear moon by night. For the first encounters of the five days' fighting, till the rain came down, Nature could not have set a fairer scene. And on the two anniversaries which have since passed, summer has again decked the battle-field. Thousands have gone out to it from Paris, from Meaux, and the whole country-side. The innumerable graves, single or grouped, among the harvest fields and the pastures, have been covered with flowers, and bright, mile after mile, with the twinkling tricolour, as far as the eye could see. At Barcy and Etrépilly, the centres of the fight, priests have blessed the graves, and prayed for the dead.

There has been neither labour nor money indeed as yet wherewith to rebuild the ruined villages and farms, beyond the most necessary repairs. They stand for the most part as the battle left them. And the fields are still alive with innumerable red flags—distinct from the tricolour of the graves—which mark where the plough must avoid an unexploded shell. In a journal of September 1914, a citizen of Senlis describes passing in a motor through the scene of the fight, immediately after the departure of the Germans, when the scavenging and burying parties were still busy.

"How can I describe it? Where to begin? Abandoned farms, on hills of death! The grain-giving earth, empty of human beings. No labourers—no household smoke. The fire of the burning villages has smouldered out, and round the houses, and in the courtyards, lie the debris of their normal life, trampled, dirty and piecemeal, under foot. Poor farms of the Ile-de-France!—dwellings of old time, into whose barns the rich harvests of the fields had been joyously gathered year by year—old tiled roofs, clothed with ancestral moss—plain hospitable rooms where masters and servants met familiarly together:—you are no more than calcined and blackened stones! Not a living animal in the ruined stalls, not an ox, not a horse, not a sheep. One flies from the houses, only to find a scene more horrible in the fields. Corpses everywhere, of men and horses. And everywhere in the fields unexploded shells, which it would be death to touch, which have already made many unsuspecting victims.

"Sometimes, as the motor draws near, a man or a woman emerges from a building, having still on their faces the terror of the hours they have lived through. They scarcely look at us. They are absorbed in their losses, in the struggle to rescue something from the wreck. As soon as they are sure it is not the Germans come back, they turn away, with slow steps, bewildered by what they have suffered."

The small party in the motor includes a priest, and as it passes near Betz, at the northern end of the battle-field, they see a burying-party of French Territorials at work. The officer in charge beckons to the priest, and the priest goes to speak to him.

"Monsieur l'Abbé, we have just buried here twenty-two French soldiers." He points to a trench freshly dug, into which the earth has just been shovelled.

"They are Breton soldiers," the officer explains, "and the men of my burying company are Bretons too. They have just discovered that these dead men we have gathered from the fields were soldiers from a regiment recruited in their own district. And *seven* of them have recognised among these twenty-two dead, one a son, one a son-in-law, one a brother. Will you come, Monsieur l'Abbé, and say a few words to these poor fellows?"

So the Abbé goes to the new-made grave, reads the *De Profundis*, says a prayer, gives the benediction, and then speaks. Tears are on the strong, rugged faces of the bare-headed Bretons, as they gather round him. A group, some little distance off, which is writing the names of the dead on a white cross, pauses, catches what is going on, and kneels too, with bent heads....

It is good to linger on that little scene of human sympathy and religious faith. It does something to protect the mind from the horror of much that has happened here.

* * * * *

In spite of the storm, our indefatigable guide carried us through all the principal points of the battle-line—St. Soupplêts—Marcilly— Barcy— Etrépilly—Acy-en-Multien; villages from which one by one, by keen, hard fighting, the French attack, coming eastwards from Dammartin to Paris, dislodged the troops of Von Kluck; while to our right lay Trocy, and Vareddes, a village on the Ourcq, between which points ran the strongest artillery positions of the enemy. At Barcy, we stopped a few minutes, to go and look at the ruined church, with its fallen bell, and its graveyard packed with wreaths and crosses, bound with the tricolour. At Etrépilly, with the snow beating in our faces, and the wind howling round us, we read the inscription on the national monument raised to those fallen in the battle, and looking eastwards to the spot where Trocy lay under thick curtains of storm, we tried to imagine the magnificent charge of the Zouaves, of the 62nd Reserve Division, under Commandant Henri D'Urbal, who, with many a comrade, lies buried in the cemetery of Barcy.

Five days the battle swayed backwards and forwards across this scene, especially following the lines of the little streams flowing eastwards to the Ourcq, the Thérouanne, the Gergogne, the Grivette. "From village to village," says Colonel Buchan, "amid the smoke of burning haystacks and farmsteads, the French bayonet attack was pressed home."

"Terrible days of life-and-death fighting! [writes a Meaux resident, Madame Koussel-Lepine] battles of Chambry, Barcy, Puisieux, Acy-en-Multien, the 6th, 7th, and 8th of September—fierce days to which the graves among the crops bear witness. Four hundred volunteers sent to attack a farm, from which only seven come back! Ambuscades, barricades in the streets, loopholes cut in the cemetery walls, trenches hastily dug and filled with dead, night fighting, often hand to hand, surprises, the sudden flash of bayonets, a rain of iron, a rain of fire, mills and houses burning like torches—fields red with the dead and with the flaming corn fruit of the fields, and flower of the race!—the sacrifice consummated, the cup drunk to the lees."

Moving and eloquent words! They gain for me a double significance as I look back from them to the little scene we saw at Barcy under the snow—a halt of some French infantry, in front of the ruined church. The "*salut an drapeau*" was going on, that simple, daily rite which, like a secular mass, is the outward and visible sign to the French soldier of his country and what he owes her. This passion of French patriotism—what a marvellous force, what a regenerating force it has shown itself in this war! It springs, too, from the heart of a race which has the Latin gift of expression. Listen to this last entry in the journal of Captain Robert Dubarle, the evening before his death in action:

"This attack to-morrow, besides the inevitable emotion it rouses in one's thoughts, stirs in me a kind of joyous impatience, and the pride of doing my duty—which is to fight gladly, and die victorious. To the last breath of our lives, to the last child of our mothers, to the last stone of our dwellings, all is thine, my country! Make no hurry. Choose thine own time for striking. If thou needest months, we will fight for months; if thou needest years, we will fight for years—the children of to-day shall be the soldiers of to-morrow.

"Already, perhaps, my last hour is hastening towards me. Accept the gift I make thee of my strength, my hopes, my joys and my sorrows, of all my being, filled with the passion of thee. Pardon thy children their errors of past days. Cover them with thy glory—put them to sleep in thy flag. Rise, victorious and renewed, upon their graves. Let our holocaust save thee—*Patrie, Patrie*!"

An utterance which for tragic sincerity and passion may well compare with the letter of an English officer I printed at the end of *England's Effort*.

On they go, into the snow and the mist, the small sturdy soldiers, bound northwards for those great and victorious attacks on the Craonne plateau, and the Chemin des Dames, which were to follow so close on our own British victory on the Vimy Ridge. They pass the two ladies in the motor car, looking at us with friendly, laughing eyes, and disappear into the storm.

Then we move on to the northern edge of the battle-field, and at Rosoy we turn south towards Meaux, passing Vareddes to our left. The weather clears a little, and from the high ground we are able to see Meaux to the west, lying beside its great river, than which our children's children will greet no more famous name. The Marne winds, steely grey, through the white landscape, and we run down to it quickly. Soon we are making our way on foot through the dripping streets of Meaux to the old bridge, which the British broke down—one of three—on their retreat—so soon to end! Then, a few minutes in the lovely cathedral—its beauty was a great surprise to me!—a greeting to the tomb of Bossuet—ah! what a *Discours* he would have written on the Battle of the Marne!—and a rapid journey of some twenty-five miles back to Paris.

But there is still a story left to tell—the story of Vareddes.

"Vareddes"—says a local historian of the battle—"is now a very quiet place. There is no movement in the streets and little life in the houses, where some of the injuries of war have been repaired." But there is no spot in the wide battlefield where there burns a more passionate hatred of a barbarous enemy. "Push open this window, enter this house, talk with any person whatever whom you may happen to meet, and they will tell you of the torture of old men, carried off as hostages and murdered in cold blood, or of the agonies of fear deliberately inflicted on old and frail women, through a whole night."

The story of Vareddes is indeed nearly incredible. That English, or French, or Italian troops could have been guilty of this particular crime is beyond imagination. Individual deeds of passion and lust are possible, indeed, in all armies, though the degree to which they have prevailed in the German army is, by the judgment of the civilised world outside Germany, unprecedented in modern history. But the instances of long-drawn-out, cold-blooded, unrelenting cruelty, of which the German conduct of the war is full, fill one after a while with a shuddering sense of something wholly vile, and wholly unsuspected, which Europe has been sheltering, unawares, in its midst. The horror has now thrown off the trappings and disguise of modern civilisation, and we see it and recoil. We feel that we are terribly right in speaking of the Germans as barbarians; that, for all their science and their organisation, they have nothing really in common with the Graeco-Latin and Christian civilisation on which this old Europe is based. We have thought of them, in former days,—how strange to look back upon it!—as brothers and co-workers in the human cause. But the men who have made and are sustaining this war, together with the men, civil and military, who have breathed its present spirit into the German Army, are really moral outlaws, acknowledging no authority but their own arrogant and cruel wills, impervious to the moral ideals and restraints that govern other nations, and betraying again and again, under the test of circumstance, the traits of the savage and the brute.

And as one says these things, one could almost laugh at them!—so strong is still the memory of what one used to feel towards the poetic, the thinking, the artistic Germany of the past. But that Germany was a mere blind, hiding the real Germany.

Listen, at least, to what this old village of the Ile-de-France knows of Germany.

With the early days of September 1914, there was a lamentable exodus from all this district. Long lines of fugitives making for safety and the south, carts filled with household stuff and carrying the women and children, herds of cattle and sheep, crowded the roads. The Germans were coming, and the terror of Belgium and the Ardennes had spread to these French peasants of the centre. On September 1st, the post-mistress of Vareddes received orders to leave the village, after destroying the telephone and telegraphic connections. The news came late, but panic spread like wildfire. All the night, Vareddes was packing and going. Of 800 inhabitants only a hundred remained, thirty of them old men.

One of the emigrants did not get far from home. He was a man of seventy, Louis Denet by name. He left Vareddes with his wife, in a farm-cart, driving a cow with them. They went a day's journey, and put up for a few days at the farm of a friend named Roger. On Sunday the 6th, in the morning, four Germans arrived at the farm. They went away and came back again in the afternoon. They called all the inmates of the farm out into the yard. Denet and Roger appeared. "You were three men this morning, now you are only two!" said one of the Germans. And immediately they took the two old men a little distance away, and shot them both, within half a mile of the farm. The body of Roger was found by his wife the day after; that of Denet was not discovered for some time. Nobody has any idea to this day why those men were shot. It is worth while to try and realise the scene—the terror-stricken old men dragged away by their murderers—the wives left behind, no doubt under a guard—the sound of the distant shots—the broken hearts of the widow and the orphan.

But that was a mere prelude.

On Friday, September 4th, a large detachment of Von Kluck's army invaded Vareddes, coming from Barcy, which lies to the west. It was no doubt moving towards the Marne on that flank march which was Von Kluck's undoing. The troops left the village on Saturday the 5th, but only to make a hurried return that same evening. Von Kluck was already aware of his danger, and was rapidly recalling troops to meet the advance of Maunoury. Meanwhile the French Sixth Army was pressing on from the west, and from the 6th to the 9th there was fierce fighting in and round Vareddes. There were German batteries behind the Presbytère, and the church had become a hospital. The old Curé, the Abbé Fossin, at the age of seventy-eight, spent himself in devoted service to the wounded Germans who filled it. There were other dressing stations near by. The Mairie, and the school, were full of wounded, of whom there were probably some hundreds in the village. Only 135 dead were buried in the neighbourhood; the Germans carried off the others in great lorries filled with corpses.

By Monday the 7th, although they were still to hold the village till the 9th, the Germans knew they were beaten. The rage of the great defeat, of the incredible disappointment, was on them. Only a week before, they had passed through the same country-side crying "Nach Paris!" and polishing up buttons, belts, rifles, accoutrements generally, so as to enter the French capital in *grande tenue*. For whatever might have been the real plans of the German General Staff, the rank and file, as they came south from Creil and Nanteuil, believed themselves only a few hours from the Boulevards, from the city of pleasure and spoil.

What had happened? The common cry of men so sharply foiled went up. "Nous sommes trahis!" The German troops in Vareddes, foreseeing immediate withdrawal, and surrounded by their own dead and dying, must somehow avenge themselves, on some one. "Hostages! The village has played us false! The Curé has been signalling from the church. We are in a nest of spies!"

So on the evening of the 7th, the old Curé, who had spent his day in the church, doing what he could for the wounded, and was worn out, had just gone to bed when there was loud knocking at his door. He was dragged out of bed, and told that he was charged with making signals to the French Army from his church tower, and so causing the defeat of the Germans.

He pointed out that he was physically incapable of climbing the tower, that any wounded German of whom the church was full could have seen him doing it, had the absurd charge been true. He reminded them that he had spent his whole time in nursing their men. No use! He is struck, hustled, spat upon, and dragged off to the Mairie. There he passed the night sitting on a hamper, and in the morning some one remembers to have seen him there, his rosary in his hand.

In one of the local accounts there is a touching photograph, taken, of course, before the war, of the Curé among the boys of the village. A mild reserved face, with something of the child in it; the face of a man who had had a gentle experience of life, and might surely hope for a gentle death.

Altogether some fourteen hostages, all but two over sixty years of age, and several over seventy, were taken during the evening and night. They ask why. The answer is, "The Germans have been betrayed!" One man is arrested because he had said to a German who was boasting that the German Army would be in Paris in two days—"All right!—but you're not there yet!" Another, because he had been seen going backwards and forwards to a wood, in which it appeared he had hidden two horses whom he had been trying to feed. One old man of seventy-nine could only walk to the yard in which the others were gathered by the help of his wife's arm. When they arrived there a soldier separated them so roughly that the wife fell.

Imagine the horror of the September night!—the terror of the women who, in the general exodus of the young and strong, had stayed behind with their husbands, the old men who could not be persuaded to leave the farms and fields in which they had spent their lives. "What harm can they do to us—old people?" No doubt that had been the instinctive feeling among those who had remained to face the invasion.

But the Germans were not content without wreaking the instinct—which is the savage instinct—to break and crush and ill-treat something which has thwarted you, on the women of Vareddes also. They gathered them out of the farmyard to which they had come, in the hopes of being allowed to stay with the men, and shut them up in a room of the farm. And there, with fixed bayonets, the soldiers amused themselves with terrifying these trembling creatures during a great part of the night. They made them all kneel down, facing a file of soldiers, and the women thought their last hour had come. One was seventy-seven years old, three sixty-seven, the two others just under sixty. The eldest, Madame Barthélemy, said to the others—"We are going to die. Make your 'contrition' if you can." (The Town Librarian of Meaux, from whose account I take these facts, heard these details from the lips of poor Madame Barthélemy herself.) The cruel scene shapes itself as we think of it—the half-lit room—the row of kneeling and weeping women, the grinning soldiers, bayonet in hand, and the old men waiting in the yard outside.

But with the morning, the French mitrailleuses are heard. The soldiers disappear.

The poor old women are free; they are able to leave their prison.

But their husbands are gone—carried off as hostages by the Germans. There were nineteen hostages in all. Three of them were taken off in a north-westerly direction, and found some German officers quartered in a château, who, after a short interrogation, released them. Of the other sixteen, fifteen were old men, and the sixteenth a child. The Curé is with them, and finds great difficulty, owing to his age, the exhaustion of the night, and lack of food, in keeping up with the column. It was now Thursday the 10th, the day following that on which, as is generally believed, the Kaiser signed the order for the general retreat of the German armies in France. But the hostages are told that the French Army has been repulsed, and the Germans will be in Paris directly.

At last the poor Curé could walk no farther. He gave his watch to a companion. "Give it to my family when you can. I am sure they mean to shoot me." Then he dropped exhausted. The Germans hailed a passing vehicle, and made him and another old man, who had fallen out, follow in it. Presently they arrive at Lizy-sur-Ourcq, through which thousands of German troops are now passing, bound not for Paris, but for Soissons and the Aisne, and in the blackest of tempers. Here, after twenty-four more hours of suffering and starvation, the Curé is brought before a court-martial of German officers sitting in a barn. He is once more charged with signalling from the church to the French Army. He again denies the charge, and reminds his judges of what he had done for the German wounded, to whose gratitude he appeals. Then four German soldiers give some sort of evidence, founded either on malice or mistake. There are no witnesses for the defence, no further inquiry. The president of the court-martial says, in bad French, to the other hostages who stand by: "The Curé has lied—he is a spy—*il sera jugé.*"

What did he mean—and what happened afterwards? The French witnesses of the scene who survived understood the officer's words to mean that the Curé would be shot. With tears, they bade him farewell, as he sat crouched in a corner of the barn guarded by two German soldiers. He was never seen again by French eyes; and the probability is that he was shot immediately after the scene in the barn.

Then the miserable march of the other old men began again. They are dragged along in the wake of the retreating Germans. The day is very hot, the roads are crowded with troops and lorries. They are hustled and hurried, and their feeble strength is rapidly exhausted. The older ones beg that they may be left to die; the younger help them as much as they can. When anyone falls out, he is kicked and beaten till he gets up again. And all the time the passing troops mock and insult them. At last, near Coulombs, after a march of two hours and a half, a man of seventy-three, called Jourdaine, falls. His guards rush upon him, with blows and kicks. In vain. He has no strength to rise, and his murderers finish him with a ball in the head and one in the side, and bury him hastily in a field a few metres off.

The weary march goes on all day. When it ends, another old man—seventy-nine years old—"le père Milliardet"—can do no more. The next morning he staggered to his feet at the order to move, but fell almost immediately. Then a soldier with the utmost coolness sent his bayonet through the heart of the helpless creature. Another falls on the road a little farther north—then another—and another. All are killed, as they lie.

The poor Maire, Liévin, struggles on as long as he can. Two other prisoners support him on either side. But he has a weak heart—his face is purple—he can hardly breathe. Again and again he falls, only to be brutally pulled up, the Germans shouting with laughter at the old man's misery. (This comes from the testimony of the survivors.) Then he, too, falls for the last time. Two soldiers take him into the cemetery of Chouy. Liévin understands, and patiently takes out his handkerchief and bandages his own eyes. It takes three balls to kill him.

Another hostage, a little farther on, who had also fallen was beaten to death before the eyes of the others.

The following day, after having suffered every kind of insult and privation, the wretched remnant of the civilian prisoners reached Soissons, and were dispatched to Germany, bound for the concentration camp at Erfurt.

Eight of them, poor souls! reached Germany, where two of them died. At last, in January 1915, four of them were returned to France through Switzerland. They reached Schaffhausen with a number of other *rapatriés,* in early February, to find there the boundless pity with which the Swiss know so well how to surround the frail and tortured sufferers of this war. In a few weeks more, they were again at home, among the old farms and woods of the Ile-de-France. "They are now in peace," says the Meaux Librarian—"among those who love them, and whose affection tries, day by day, to soften for them the cruel memory of their Calvary and their exile."

A monument to the memory of the murdered hostages is to be erected in the village market-place, and a *plaque* has been let into the wall of the farm where the old men and the women passed their first night of agony.

* * * * *

What is the moral of this story? I have chosen it to illustrate again the historic words which should be, I think—and we know that what is in our hearts is in your hearts also!—the special watchword of the Allies and of America, in these present days, when the German strength *may* collapse at any moment, and the problems of peace negotiations *may* be upon us before we know.

Reparation—Restitution—Guarantees!

The story of Vareddes, like that of Senlis, is not among the vilest—by a long, long way—of those which have steeped the name of Germany in eternal infamy during this war. The tale of Gerbéviller—which I shall take for my third instance—as I heard it from the lips of eye-witnesses, plunges us in deeper depths of horror; and the pages of the Bryce report are full of incidents beside which that of Vareddes looks almost colourless.

All the same, let us insist again that no Army of the Allies, or of America, or of any British Dominion, would have been capable of the treatment given by the soldiers of Germany to the hostages of Vareddes. It brings out into sharp relief that quality, or "mentality," to use the fashionable word, which Germany shares with Austria—witness the Austrian doings in Serbia—and with Turkey—witness Turkey's doings in Armenia—but not with any other civilised nation. It is the quality of, or the tendency to, deliberate and pitiless cruelty; a quality which makes of the man or nation who shows it a particularly terrible kind of animal force; and the more terrible, the more educated. Unless we can put it down and stamp it out, as it has become embodied in a European nation, European freedom and peace, American freedom and peace, have no future.

But now, let me carry you to Lorraine!—to the scenes of that short but glorious campaign of September 1914, by which, while the Battle of the Marne was being fought, General Castelnau was protecting the right of the French armies; and to the devastated villages where American kindness is already at work, rebuilding the destroyed, and comforting the broken-hearted.

No. 9

May 24th, 1917.

DEAR MR. ROOSEVELT,—To any citizen of a country allied with France in the present struggle, above all to any English man or woman who is provided with at least some general knowledge of the Battle of the Marne, the journey across France from Paris to Nancy can never fail to be one of poignant interest. Up to a point beyond Châlons, the "Ligne de l'Est" follows in general the course of the great river, and therefore the line of the battle. You pass La Fertée-sous-Jouarre, where the Third Corps of General French's army crossed the river; Charly-sur-Marne, where a portion of the First Corps found an unexpectedly easy crossing, owing, it is said, to the hopeless drunkenness of the enemy rear-guard charged with defending the bridge; and Château Thierry, famous in the older history of France, where the right of the First Corps crossed after sharp fighting, and, in the course of "a gigantic man-hunt" in and around the town, took a large number of German prisoners, before, by nightfall, coming into touch with the left of the French Fifth Army under Franchet d'Espercy. At Dornans you are only a few miles north of the Marshes of St. Gond, where General Foch, after some perilous moments, won his brilliant victory over General Billow and the German Second Army, including a corps of the Prussian Guards; while at Châlons I look up from a record I am reading of the experiences of the Diocese during the war, written by the Bishop, to watch for the distant cathedral, and recall the scene of the night of September 9th, when the German Headquarters Staff in that town, "flown with insolence and wine," after what is described as "an excellent dinner and much riotous drinking," were roused about midnight by a sudden noise in the Hôtel, and shouts of "The French are here!" "In fifteen minutes," writes an officer of the Staff of General Langle de Gary, "the Hôtel was empty."

At Épernay and Châlons those French officers who were bound for the fighting line in Champagne, east and west of Reims, left the train; and somewhere beyond Épernay I followed in thought the flight of an aeroplane which seemed to be heading northwards across the ridges which bound the river valley—northwards for Reims, and that tragic ghost which the crime of Germany has set moving through history for ever, never to be laid or silenced—Joan of Arc's Cathedral. Then, at last, we are done with the Marne. We pass Bar-le-Duc, on one of her tributaries, the Ornain; after which the splendid Meuse flashes into sight, running north on its victorious way to Verdun; then the Moselle, with Toul and its beautiful church on the right; and finally the Meurthe, on which stands Nancy. A glorious sisterhood of rivers! The more one realises what they have meant to the history of France, the more one understands that strong instinct of the early Greeks, which gave every river its god, and made of the Simois and the Xanthus personages almost as real as Achilles himself.

But alas! the whole great spectacle, here as on the Ourcq, was sorely muffled and blurred by the snow, which lay thick over the whole length and breadth of France, effacing the landscape in one monotonous whiteness. If I remember rightly, however, it had ceased to fall, and twenty-four hours after we reached Nancy, it had disappeared. It lasted just long enough to let us see the fairy-like Place Stanislas raise its beautiful gilded gates and white palaces between the snow and the moon-light—a sight not soon forgotten.

We were welcomed at Nancy by the Préfet of the Department, Monsieur Léon Mirman, to whom an old friend had written from Paris, and by the courteous French officer, Capitaine de B., who was to take us in charge, for the French Army, during our stay. M. Mirman and his active and public-spirited wife have done a great work at Nancy, and in the desolated country round it. From the ruined villages of the border, the poor *réfugiés* have been gathered into the old capital of Lorraine, and what seemed to me a remarkably efficient and intelligent philanthropy has been dealing with their needs and those of their children. Nor is this all. M. Mirman is an old Radical and of course a Government official, sent down some years ago from Paris. Lorraine is ardently Catholic, as we all know, and her old Catholic families are not the natural friends of the Republican *régime*. But President Poincaré's happy phrase, *l'union sacrée*—describing the fusion of all parties, classes, and creeds in the war service of France, has nowhere found a stronger echo than in Lorraine. The Préfet is on the friendliest of terms with the Catholic population, rich and poor; and they, on their side, think and speak warmly of a man who is clearly doing his patriotic best for all alike.

Our first day's journeyings were to show us something of the qualities of this Catholic world of Lorraine. A charming and distinguished Frenchwoman who accompanied us counted, no doubt, for much in the warmth of the kindness shown us. And yet I like to believe—indeed I am sure—that there was more than this in it. There was the thrilling sense of a friendship between our two nations, a friendship new and far-reaching, cemented by the war, but looking beyond it, which seemed to me to make the background of it all. Long as I have loved and admired the French, I have often—like many others of their English friends and admirers—felt and fretted against the kind of barrier that seemed to exist between their intimate life and ours. It was as though, at bottom, and in the end, something cold and critical in the French temperament, combined with ignorance and prejudice on our own part, prevented a real contact between the two nationalities. In Lorraine, at any rate, and for the first time, I felt this "something" gone. Let us only carry forward *intelligently*, after the war, the process of friendship born from the stress and anguish of this time—for there is an art and skill in friendship, just as there is an art and skill in love—and new horizons will open for both nations. The mutual respect, the daily intercourse, and the common glory of our two armies fighting amid the fields and woods of France—soon to welcome a third army, your own, to their great fellowship!— are the foundations to-day of all the rest; and next come the efforts that have been made by British and Americans to help the French in remaking and rebuilding their desolated land, efforts that bless him that gives and him that takes, but especially him that gives; of which I shall have more to say in the course of this letter. But a common victory, and a common ardour in rebuilding the waste places, and binding up the broken-hearted: even they will not be enough, unless, beyond the war, all three nations, nay, all the Allies, do not set themselves to a systematic interpenetration of life and thought, morally, socially, commercially. As far as France and England are concerned, English people must go more to France; French people must come more to England. Relations of hospitality, of correspondence, of wide mutual acquaintance, must not be left to mere chance; they must be furthered by the mind of both nations. Our English children must go for part of their education to France; and French children must be systematically wooed over here. Above all the difficulty of language must be tackled as it has never been yet, so that it may be a real disadvantage and disgrace for the boy or girl of either country who has had a secondary education not to be able to speak, in some fashion, the language of the other. As for the working classes, and the country populations of both countries, what they have seen of each other, as brothers in arms during the war, may well prove of more lasting importance than anything else.

* * * * *

But I am wandering a little from Nancy, and the story of our long Sunday. The snow had disappeared, and there were voices of spring in the wind. A French Army motor arrived early, with another French officer, the Capitaine de G——, who proved to be a most interesting and stimulating guide. With him I drove slowly through the beautiful town, looking at the ruined houses, which are fairly frequent in its streets. For Nancy has had its bombardments, and there is one gun of long range in particular, surnamed by the town—"la grosse Bertha," which has done, and still does, at intervals, damage of the kind the German loves. Bombs, too, have been dropped by aeroplanes both here and at Lunéville, in streets crowded with non-combatants, with the natural result. It has been in reprisal for this and similar deeds elsewhere, and in the hope of stopping them, that the French have raided German towns across the frontier. But the spirit of Nancy remains quite undaunted. The children of its schools, drilled to run down to the cellars at the first alarm as our children are drilled to empty a school on a warning of a Zeppelin raid, are the gayest and most spirited creatures, as I saw them at their games and action songs; unless indeed it be the children of the *réfugiés*, in whose faces sometimes one seems to see the reflection of scenes that no child ought to have witnessed and not even a child can forget. For these children come from the frontier villages, ravaged by the German advance, and still, some of them, in German occupation. And the orgy of murder, cruelty, and arson which broke out at No16ny, Badonviller, and Gerbéviller, during the campaign of 1914, has scarcely been surpassed elsewhere—even in Belgium. Here again, as at Vareddes, the hideous deeds done were largely owing to the rage of defeat. The Germans, mainly Bavarians, on the frontier, had set their hearts on Nancy, as the troops of Von Kluck had set their hearts on Paris; and

68

General Castelnau, commanding the Second Army, denied them Nancy, as Maunoury's Sixth Army denied Paris to Von Kluck.

But more of this presently. We started first of all for a famous point in the fighting of 1914, the farm and hill of Léomont. By this time the day had brightened into a cold sunlight, and as we sped south from Nancy on the Lunéville road, through the old town of St. Nicholas du Port, with its remarkable church, and past the great salt works at Dombasle, all the country-side was clear to view.

Good fortune indeed!—as I soon discovered when, after climbing a steep hill to the east of the road, we found ourselves in full view of the fighting lines and a wide section of the frontier, with the Forest of Parroy, which is still partly German, stretching its dark length southward on the right, while to the north ran the famous heights of the Grand Couronné;—name of good omen!—which suggests so happily the historical importance of the ridge which protects Nancy and covers the French right. Then, turning westward, one looked over the valley of the Meurthe, with its various tributaries, the Mortagne in particular, on which stands Gerbéviller; and away to the Moselle and the Meuse. But the panoramic view was really made to live and speak for me by the able man at my side. With French precision and French logic, he began with the geography of the country, its rivers and hills and plateaux, and its natural capacities for defence against the German enemy; handling the view as though it had been a great map, and pointing out, as he went, the disposition of the French frontier armies, and the use made of this feature and that by the French generals in command.

This Lorraine Campaign, at the opening of the war, is very little realised outside France. It lasted some three weeks. It was preceded by the calamitous French reverse at Morhange, where, on August 20th, portions of the 15th and 16th Corps of the Second Army, young troops drawn from south-western France—who in subsequent actions fought with great bravery—broke in rout before a tremendous German attack. The defeat almost gave the Germans Nancy. But General Castelnau and General Foch, between them, retrieved the disaster. They fell back on Nancy and the line of the Mortagne, while the Germans, advancing farther south, occupied Luneville (August 22nd) and burnt Gerbéviller. On the 23rd, 24th, and 25th there was fierce fighting on and near this hill on which we stood. Capitaine de G—— with the 2nd Battalion of Chausseurs, under General Dubail, had been in the thick of the struggle, and he described to me the action on the slopes beneath us, and how, through his glasses, he had watched the enemy on the neighbouring hill forcing parties of French civilians to bury the German dead and dig German trenches, under the fire of their own people.

The hill of Léomont, and the many graves upon it, were quiet enough as we stood talking there. The old farm was in ruins; and in the fields stretching up the hill there were the remains of trenches. All around and below us spread the beautiful Lorraine country, with its rivers and forests; and to the south-east one could just see the blue mass of Mont Donon, and the first spurs of the Vosges.

"Can you show me exactly where the French line runs?" I asked my companion. He pointed to a patch of wood some six miles away. "There is a

French battalion there. And you see that other patch of wood a little farther east? There is a German battalion there. Ah!" Suddenly he broke off, and the younger officer with us, Capitaine de B——, came running up, pointing overhead. I craned my neck to look into the spring blue above us, and there—7,000 to 8,000 feet high, according to the officers—were three Boche aeroplanes pursued by two French machines. In and out a light band of white cloud, the fighters in the air chased each other, shrapnel bursting all round them like tufts of white wool. They were so high that they looked mere white specks. Yet we could follow their action perfectly—how the Germans climbed, before running for home, and how the French pursued! It was breathless while it lasted! But we did not see the end. The three Taubes were clearly driven back; and in a few seconds they and the Frenchmen had disappeared in distance and cloud towards the fighting-line. The following day, at a point farther to the north, a well-known French airman was brought down and killed, in just such a fight.

Beyond Léomont we diverged westward from the main road, and found ourselves suddenly in one of those utterly ruined villages which now bestrew the soil of Northern, Central, and Eastern France; of that France which has been pre-eminently for centuries, in spite of revolutions, the pious and watchful guardian of what the labour of dead generations has bequeathed to their sons. Vitrimont, however, was destroyed in fair fight during the campaign of 1914. Bombardment had made wreck of the solid houses, built of the warm red stone of the country. It had destroyed the church, and torn up the graveyard; and when its exiled inhabitants returned to it by degrees, even French courage and French thrift quailed before the task of reconstruction. But presently there arrived a quiet American lady, who began to make friends with the people of Vitrimont, to find out what they wanted, and to consult with all those on the spot who could help to bring the visions in her mind to pass,—with the Préfet, with the officials, local and governmental, of the neighbouring towns, with the Catholic women of the richer Lorraine families, gentle, charitable, devout, who quickly perceived her quality, and set themselves to co-operate with her. It was the American lady's intention—simply—to rebuild Vitrimont. And she is steadily accomplishing it, with the help of generous money subsidies coming, month by month, from one rich American woman—a woman of San Francisco—across the Atlantic. How one envies that American woman!

The sight of Miss Polk at work lives indeed, a warm memory, in one's heart. She has established herself in two tiny rooms in a peasant's cottage, which have been made just habitable for her. A few touches of bright colour, a picture or two, a book or two, some flowers, with furniture of the simplest—amid these surroundings on the outskirts of the ruined village, with one of its capable, kindly faced women to run the *ménage*, Miss Polk lives and works, realising bit by bit the plans of the new Vitrimont, which have been drawn for her by the architect of the department, and following loyally old Lorraine traditions. The church has been already restored and reopened. The first mass within its thronged walls was—so the spectators say—a moving sight. "*That sad word— Joy*"—Landor's pregnant phrase comes back to one, as expressing the bitter-sweet of all glad things in this countryside, which has seen—so short a time

70

ago—death and murder and outrage at their worst. The gratitude of the villagers to their friend and helper has taken various forms. The most public mark of it, so far, has been Miss Folk's formal admission to the burgess rights of Vitrimont, which is one of the old communes of France. And the village insists that she shall claim her rights! When the time came for dividing the communal wood in the neighbouring forest, her fellow citizens arrived to take her with them and show her how to obtain her share. As to the affection and confidence with which she is regarded, it was enough to walk with her through the village, to judge of its reality.

But it makes one happy to think that it is not only Americans who have done this sort of work in France. Look, for instance, at the work of the Society of Friends in the department of the Marne,—on that fragment of the battlefield which extends from Bar-le-Duc to Vitry St. François. "Go and ask," wrote a French writer in 1915, "for the village of Huiron, or that of Glannes, or that other, with its name to shudder at, splashed with blood and powder—Sermaize. Inquire for the English Quakers. Books, perhaps, have taught you to think of them as people with long black coats and long faces. Where are they? Here are only a band of workmen, smooth-faced—not like our country folk. They laugh and sing while they make the shavings fly under the plane and the saw. They are building wooden houses, and roofing them with tiles. Around them are poor people whose features are stiff and grey like those of the dead. These are the women, the old men, the children, the weaklings of our sweet France, who have lived for months in damp caves and dens, till they look like Lazarus rising from the tomb. But life is beginning to come back to their eyes and their lips. The hands they stretch out to you tremble with joy. To-night they will sleep in a house, in *their* house. And inside there will be beds and tables and chairs, and things to cook with.... As they go in and look, they embrace each other, sobbing."

By June 1915, 150 "Friends" had rebuilt more than 400 houses, and rehoused more than seven hundred persons. They had provided ploughs and other agricultural gear, seeds for the harvest fields and for the gardens, poultry for the farmyards. And from that day to this, the adorable work has gone on. "*By this shall all men know that ye are My disciples, if ye love one another.*"

* * * * *

It is difficult to tear oneself away from themes like this, when the story one has still to tell is the story of Gerbéviller. At Vitrimont the great dream of Christianity—the City of God on earth—seems still reasonable.

At Hérémenil, and Gerbéviller, we are within sight and hearing of deeds that befoul the human name, and make one despair of a world in which they can happen.

At luncheon in a charming house of old Lorraine, with an intellectual and spiritual atmosphere that reminded me of a book that was one of the abiding joys of my younger days—the *Récit d'une Soeur*—we heard from the lips of some of those present an account of the arrival at Lunéville of the fugitives from Gerbéviller, after the entry of the Bavarians into the town. Women and children and old men, literally mad with terror, had escaped from the burning town, and found their way over the thirteen kilomètres that separate Gerbéviller from Lunéville. No intelligible account could be got from them; they had seen things that shatter the nerves and brain of the weak and old; they were scarcely human in their extremity of fear. And when, an hour later, we ourselves reached Gerbéviller, the terror which had inspired that frenzied flight became, as we listened to Soeur Julie, a tangible presence haunting the ruined town.

Gerbéviller and Soeur Julie are great names in France to-day. Gerbéviller, with No. ény, Badonviller, and Sermaize, stand in France for what is most famous in German infamy; Soeur Julie, the "chère soeur" of so many narratives, for that form of courage and whole-hearted devotion which is specially dear to the French, because it has in it a touch of *panache*, of audacity! It is not too meek; it gets its own back when it can, and likes to punish the sinner as well as to forgive him. Sister Julie of the Order of St. Charles of Nancy, Madame Rigard, in civil parlance, had been for years when the war broke out the head of a modest cottage hospital in the small country town of Gerbéviller. The town was prosperous and pretty; its gardens ran down to the Mortagne flowing at its feet, and it owned a country house in a park, full of treasures new and old— tapestries, pictures, books—as Lorraine likes to have such things about her.

But unfortunately, it occupied one of the central points of the fighting in the campaign of Lorraine, after the defeat of General Castelnau's Army at Morhange on August 20th, 1914. The exultant and victorious Germans pushed on rapidly after that action. Lunéville was occupied, and the fighting spread to the districts south and west of that town. The campaign, however, lasted only three weeks, and was determined by the decisive French victory of September 8th on the Grand Couronné. By September 12th Nancy was safe; Lunéville and Gerbéviller had been retaken; and the German line had been driven back to where we saw it from the hill of Léomont. But in that three weeks a hell of cruelty, in addition to all the normal sufferings of war, had been let loose on the villages of Lorraine; on No/mény to the north of Nancy, on Badonviller, Baccarat, and Gerbéviller to the south. The Bavarian troops, whose record is among the worst in the war, got terribly out of hand, especially when the tide turned against them; and if there is one criminal who, if he is still living, will deserve and, I hope, get an impartial trial some day before an international tribunal, it will be the Bavarian General, General Clauss.

Here is the first-hand testimony of M. Mirman, the Prefét of the Department. At Gerbeviller, he writes, the ruin and slaughter of the town and its inhabitants had nothing to do with legitimate war:

"We are here in presence of an inexpiable crime. The crime was signed. Such signatures are soon rubbed out. I saw that of the murderer—and I bear my testimony.

"The bandits who were at work here were assassins: I have seen the bodies of their victims, and taken the evidence on the spot. They shot down the inhabitants like rabbits, killing them haphazard in the streets, on their doorsteps, almost at arm's length. Of these victims it is still difficult to ascertain the exact number; it will be more than fifty. Most of the victims had been buried when I first entered

72

the town; here and there, however, in a garden, at the entrance to a cellar the corpses of women still awaited burial. In a field just outside the town, I saw on the ground, their hands tied, some with their eyes bandaged—fifteen old men—murdered. They were in three groups of five. The men of each group had evidently clung to each other before death. The clenched hand of one of them still held an old pipe. They were all old men—with white hair. Some days had elapsed since their murder; but their aspect in death was still venerable; their quiet closed eyes seemed to appeal to heaven. A staff officer of the Second Army who was with me photographed the scene; with other *pièces de conviction*; the photograph is in the hands of the Governmental Commission charged with investigating the crimes of the Germans during this war."

The Bavarian soldiers in Gerbéviller were not only murderers—they were incendiaries, even more deliberate and thorough-going than the soldiers of Von Kluck's army at Senlis. With the exception of a few houses beyond the hospital, spared at the entreaty of Soeur Julie, and on her promise to nurse the German wounded, the whole town was deliberately burnt out, house by house, the bare walls left standing, the rest destroyed. And as, *after the fire*, the place was twice taken and retaken under bombardment, its present condition may be imagined. It was during the burning that some of the worst murders and outrages took place. For there is a maddening force in triumphant cruelty, which is deadlier than that of wine; under it men become demons, and all that is human perishes.

The excuse, of course, was here as at Senlis—"les civils ont tiré!" There is not the slightest evidence in support of the charge. As at Senlis, there was a French rear-guard of 57 Chasseurs—left behind to delay the German advance as long as possible. They were told to hold their ground for five hours; they held it for eleven, fighting with reckless bravery, and firing from a street below the hospital. The Germans, taken by surprise, lost a good many men before, at small loss to themselves, the Chasseurs retreated. In their rage at the unexpected check, and feeling, no doubt, already that the whole campaign was going against them, the Germans avenged themselves on the town and its helpless inhabitants.

Our half-hour in Soeur Julie's parlour was a wonderful experience! Imagine a portly woman of sixty, with a shrewd humorous face, talking with French vivacity, and with many homely turns of phrase drawn straight from that life of the soil and the peasants amid which she worked; a woman named in one of General Castelnau's Orders of the Day and entitled to wear the Legion of Honour; a woman, too, who has seen horror face to face as few women, even in war, have seen it, yet still simple, racy, full of irony, and full of heart, talking as a mother might talk of her "grands blessés"! but always with humorous asides, and an utter absence of pose or pretence; flashing now into scorn and now into tenderness, as she described the conduct of the German officers who searched her hospital for arms, or the helplessness of the wounded men whom she protected. I will try and put down some of her talk. It threw much light for me on the psychology of two nations.

"During the fighting, we had always about 300 of our wounded (*nos chers blessés*) in this hospital. As fast as we sent them off, others came in. All our stores were soon exhausted. I was thankful we had some good wine in the cellars—about 200 bottles. You understand, Madame, that when we go to nurse our people in their farms, they don't pay us, but they like to give us something—very often it is a bottle of old wine, and we put it in the cellar, when it comes in handy often for our invalids. Ah! I was glad of it for our *blessés*! I said to my Sisters—'Give it them! and not by thimblefuls—give them enough!' Ah, poor things!—it made some of them sleep. It was all we had. One day, I passed a soldier who was lying back in his bed with a sigh of satisfaction. '*Ah, ma Soeur, ça resusciterait un mort!*' (That would bring a dead man to life!) So I stopped to ask what they had just given him. And it was a large glass of Lachryma Christi!

"But then came the day when the Commandant, the French Commandant, you understand, came to me and said—'Sister, I have sad news for you. I am going. I am taking away the wounded—and all my stores. Those are my orders.'

"'But, mon Commandant, you'll leave me some of your stores for the grands blessés, whom you leave behind—whom you can't move? *What!*—you must take it all away? Ah, ça—*non*! I don't want any extras—I won't take your chloroform—I won't take your bistouris—I won't take your electric things—but—hand over the iodine! (*en avant l'iode*!) hand over the cotton-wool!—hand over the gauze! Come, my Sisters!' I can tell you I plundered him!—and my Sisters came with their aprons, and the linen-baskets—we carried away all we could."

Then she described the evacuation of the French wounded at night—300 of them—all but the 19 worst cases left behind. There were no ambulances, no proper preparation of any kind.

"Oh! it was a confusion!—an ugly business!" (*ce n'etait pas rose!*). The Sisters tore down and split up the shutters, the doors, to serve as stretchers; they tore sheets into long strips and tied "our poor children" on to the shutters, and hoisted them into country carts of every sort and description. "Quick!—Quick!" She gave us a wonderful sense of the despairing haste in which the night retreat had to be effected. All night their work went on. The wounded never made a sound—"they let us do what we would without a word. And as for us, my Sisters bound these big fellows (*ces gros et grands messieurs*) on to the improvised stretchers, like a mother who fastens her child in its cot. Ah! Jésus! the poverty and the misery of that time!"

By the early morning all the French wounded were gone except the nineteen helpless cases, and all the French soldiers had cleared out of the village except the 57 Chasseurs, whose orders were to hold the place as long as they could, to cover the retreat of the rest.

Then, when the Chasseurs finally withdrew, the Bavarian troops rushed up the town in a state of furious excitement, burning it systematically as they advanced, and treating the inhabitants as M. Mirman has described. Soon Soeur Julie knew that they were coming up the hill towards the hospital. I will quote the very language—homely, Biblical, direct—in which she described her feelings. "*Mes reins flottaient comme ça—ils allaient tomber à mes talons. Instantanément, pas une goutte de salive dans la bouche!*" Or—to translate it in the weaker English

74

idiom—"My heart went down into my heels—all in a moment, my mouth was dry as a bone!"

The German officers drew up, and asked for the Superior of the hospital. She went out to meet them. Here she tried to imitate the extraordinary arrogance of the German manner.

"They told me they would have to burn the hospital, as they were informed men had been shooting from it at their troops.

"I replied that if anyone had been shooting, it was the French Chasseurs, who were posted in a street close by, and had every right to shoot!"

At last they agreed to let the hospital alone, and burn no more houses, if she would take in the German wounded. So presently the wards of the little hospital were full again to overflowing. But while the German wounded were coming in the German officers insisted on searching the nineteen French wounded for arms.

"I had to make way for them—I *had* to say, '*Entrez, Messieurs!*'"

Then she dropped her voice, and said between her teeth—"Think how hard that was for a Lorrainer!"

So two German officers went to the ward where the nineteen Frenchmen lay, all helpless cases, and a scene followed very like that in the hospital at Senlis. One drew his revolver and covered the beds, the other walked round, poniard in hand, throwing back the bedclothes to look for arms. But they found nothing—"*only blood*! For we had had neither time enough nor dressings enough to treat the wounds properly that night."

A frightful moment!—the cowering patients—the officers in a state of almost frenzied excitement, searching bed after bed. At the last bed, occupied by a badly wounded and quite helpless youth, the officer carrying the dagger brought the blade of it so near to the boy's throat that Soeur Julie rushed forward, and placed her two hands in front of the poor bare neck. The officer dropped both arms to his side, she said, "as if he had been shot," and stood staring at her, quivering all over. But from that moment she had conquered them.

For the German wounded, Soeur Julie declared she had done her best, and the officer in charge of them afterwards wrote her a letter of thanks. Then her mouth twisted a little. "But I wasn't—well, I didn't *spoil* them! (*Je n'étais pas trop tendre*); I didn't give them our best wine!" And one officer whose wounds she dressed, a Prussian colonel who never deigned to speak to a Bavarian captain near him, was obliged to accept a good many home truths from her. He was convinced that she would poison his leg unless he put on the dressings himself. But he allowed her to bandage him afterwards. During this operation—which she hinted she had performed in a rather Spartan fashion!—"he whimpered all the time," and she was able to give him a good deal of her mind on the war and the behaviour of his troops. He and the others, she said, were always talking about their Kaiser; "one might have thought they saw him sitting on the clouds."

In two or three days the French returned victorious, to find the burnt and outraged village. The Germans were forced, in their turn, to leave some badly wounded men behind, and the French *poilus* in their mingled wrath and exultation could not resist, some of them, abusing the German wounded through the windows of the hospital. But then, with a keen dramatic instinct, Soeur Julie drew a striking picture of the contrast between the behaviour of the French officer going down to the basement to visit the wounded German officers there, and that of the German officers on a similar errand. She conveyed with perfect success the cold civility of the Frenchman, beginning with a few scathing words about the treatment of the town, and then proceeding to an investigation of the personal effects of the Boche officers.

"Your papers, gentlemen? Ah! those are private letters—you may retain them. Your purses?"—he looks at them—"I hand them back to you. Your note-books? *Ah! ça—c'est mon affaire!* (that's my business). I wish you good morning."

Soeur Julie spoke emphatically of the drunkenness of the Germans. They discovered a store of "Mirabelle," a strong liqueur, in the town, and had soon exhausted it, with apparently the worst results.

Well!—the March afternoon ran on, and we could have sat there listening till dusk. But our French officers were growing a little impatient, and one of them gently drew "the dear sister," as every one calls her, towards the end of her tale. Then with regret one left the plain parlour, the little hospital which had played so big a part, and the brave elderly nun, in whom one seemed to see again some of those qualities which, springing from the very soil of Lorraine, and in the heart of a woman, had once, long years ago, saved France.

* * * * *

How much there would be still to say about the charm and the kindness of Lorraine, if only this letter were not already too long! But after the tragedy of Gerbéviller I must at any rate find room for the victory of Amance.

Alas!—the morning was dull and misty when we left Nancy for Amance and the Grand Couronné; so that when we stood at last on the famous ridge immediately north of the town which saw, on September 8th, 1914, the wrecking of the final German attempt on Nancy, there was not much visible except the dim lines of forest and river in the plain below. Our view ought to have ranged as far, almost, as Metz to the north and the Vosges to the south. But at any rate there, at our feet, lay the Forest of Champenoux, which was the scene of the three frantic attempts of the Germans debouching from it on September 8th to capture the hill of Amance, and the plateau on which we stood. Again and again the 75's on the hill mowed down the advancing hordes and the heavy guns behind completed their work. The Germans broke and fled, never to return. Nancy was saved, the right of the six French Armies advancing across France, at that very moment, on the heels of the retreating Germans, in the Battle of the Marne, was protected thereby from a flank attack which might have altered all the fortunes of the war, and the course of history; and General Castelnau had written his name on the memory of Europe.

But—the Kaiser was not there! Even Colonel Buchan in his admirable history of the war, and Major Whitton in his recent book on the campaign of the Marne, repeat the current legend. I can only bear witness that the two French staff officers who walked with us along the Grand Couronné—one of whom had been in the battle of September 8th—were positive that the Kaiser was not in the neighbourhood at the time, and that there was no truth at all in the famous story which describes him as watching the battle from the edge of the Forest of Champenoux, and riding off ahead of his defeated troops, instead of making, as he had reckoned, a triumphant entry into Nancy. Well, it is a pity the gods did not order it so!—"to be a tale for those that should come after."

One more incident before we leave Lorraine! On our way up to the high village of Amance, we had passed some three or four hundred French soldiers at work. They looked with wide eyes of astonishment at the two ladies in the military car. When we reached the village, Prince R——, the young staff officer from a neighbouring Headquarters who was to meet us there, had not arrived, and we spent some time in a cottage, chatting with the women who lived in it. Then—apparently—while we were on the ridge word reached the men working below, from the village, that we were English. And on the drive down we found them gathered, three or four hundred, beside the road, and as we passed them they cheered us heartily, seeing in us, for the moment, the British alliance!

So that we left the Grand Couronné with wet eyes, and hearts all passionate sympathy towards Lorraine and her people.

No. 10

June 1st, 1917.

DEAR MR. ROOSEVELT,—In looking back over my two preceding letters, I realise how inadequately they express the hundredth part of that vast and insoluble debt of a guilty Germany to an injured France, the realisation of which became—for me—in Lorraine, on the Ourcq, and in Artois, a burning and overmastering thing, from which I was rarely or never free. And since I returned to England on March 16th, the conduct of the German troops, under the express orders of the German Higher Command, in the French districts evacuated since February by Hindenburg's retreating forces, has only sharpened and deepened the judgment of civilised men, with regard to the fighting German and all his ways, which has been formed long since, beyond alteration or recall.

Think of it! It cries to heaven. Think of Reims and Arras, of Verdun and Ypres, think of the hundreds of towns and villages, the thousands of individual houses and farms, that lie ruined on the old soil of France; think of the sufferings of the helpless and the old, the hideous loss of life, of stored-up wealth, of natural and artistic beauty; and then let us ask ourselves again the old, old question—why has this happened? And let us go back again to the root facts, from which, whenever he or she considers them afresh—and they should be constantly considered afresh—every citizen of the Allied nations can only draw fresh courage to endure. The long and passionate preparation for war in Germany; the half-mad literature of a glorified "force" headed by the Bernhardis and Treitschkes, and repeated by a thousand smaller folk, before the war; the far more illuminating manifestoes of the intellectuals since the war; Germany's refusal of a conference, as proposed and pressed by Great Britain, in the week before August 4th, France's acceptance of it; Germany's refusal to respect the Belgian neutrality to which she had signed her name, France's immediate consent; the provisions of mercy and of humanity signed by Germany in the Hague Convention trampled, almost with a sneer, under foot; the jubilation over the *Lusitania*, and the arrogant defence of all that has been most cruel and most criminal in the war, as necessary to Germany's interests, and therefore moral, therefore justified; let none—none!—of these things rest forgotten in our minds until peace is here, and justice done!

The German armies are capable of "*no undisciplined cruelty*," said the 93 Professors, without seeing how damning was the phrase. No!—theirs was a cruelty by order, meditated, organised, and deliberate. The stories of Senlis, of Vareddes, of Gerbéviller which I have specially chosen, as free from that element of sexual horror which repels many sensitive people from even trying to realise what has happened in this war, are evidences—one must insist again—of a national mind and quality, with which civilised Europe and civilised America can make no truce. And what folly lies behind the wickedness! Let me recall to American readers some of the phrases in the report of your former Minister in Belgium—Mr. Brand Whitlock—on the Belgian deportations, the "slave hunts" that Germany has carried out in Belgium and "which have torn from nearly every humble home in the land, a husband, father, son, or brother."

These proceedings [says Mr. Whitlock] place in relief the German capacity for blundering almost as sharply as the German capacity for cruelty. They have destroyed for generations any hope whatever of friendly relations between themselves and the Belgian people. For these things were done not, as with the early atrocities, in the heat of passion and the first lust of war, but by one of those deeds that make one despair of the future of the human race—a deed coldly planned, studiously matured, and deliberately and systematically executed, a deed so cruel that German soldiers are said to have wept in its execution, and so monstrous that even German officers are now said to be ashamed.

But the average German neither weeps nor blames. He is generally amazed, when he is not amused, by the state of feeling which such proceedings excite. And if he is an "intellectual," a professor, he will exhaust himself in ingenious and utterly callous defences of all that Germany has done or may do. An astonishing race—the German professors! The year before the war there was an historical congress in London. There was a hospitality committee, and my husband and I were asked to entertain some of the learned men. I remember one in particular—an old man with white hair, who with his wife and daughter joined the party after dinner. His name was Professor Otto von Gierke of the University of Berlin. I gathered from his conversation that he and his family had been very kindly entertained in London. His manner was somewhat harsh and over-bearing, but his white hair and spectacles gave him a venerable aspect, and it was clear that he and his wife and daughter belonged to a cultivated and intelligent *milieu*. But who among his English hosts could possibly have imagined the thoughts and ideas in that grey head? I find a speech of his in a most illuminating book by a Danish professor on German Chauvinist literature. [*Hurrah and Hallelujah!* By J. P. Bang, D.D., Professor of Theology at the University of Copenhagen, translated by Jessie Bröchner.] The speech was published in a collection called *German Speeches in Hard Times*, which contains names once so distinguished as those of Von Wilamovitz and Harnack.

Professor von Gierke's effusion begins with the usual German falsehoods as to the origin of the war, and then continues—"But now that we Germans are plunged in war, we will have it in *all its grandeur and violence*! Neither fear nor *pity* shall stay our arm before it has completely brought our enemies to the ground." They shall be reduced to such a condition that they shall never again dare even to snarl at Germany. Then German Kultur will show its full loveliness and strength, enlightening "the understanding of the foreign races absorbed and incorporated into the Empire, and making them see that only from German kultur can they derive those treasures which they need for their own particular life."

At the moment when these lines were written—for the book was published early in the war—the orgy of murder and lust and hideous brutality which had swept through Belgium in the first three weeks of the war was beginning to be known in England; the traces of it were still fresh in town after town and village after village of that tortured land; while the testimony of its victims was just beginning to be sifted by the experts of the Bryce Commission.

The hostages of Vareddes, the helpless victims of Nomény, of Gerbéviller, of Sermaize, of Sommeilles, and a score of other places in France were scarcely cold in their graves. But the old white-haired professor stands there, unashamed, unctuously offering the kultur of his criminal nation to an expectant world! "And when the victory is won," he says complacently—"the whole world will stand open to us, our war expenses will be paid by the vanquished, the black-white-and-red flag will wave over all seas; our countrymen will hold highly respected posts in all parts of the world, and we shall maintain and extend our colonies."

God, forbid! So says the whole English-speaking race, you on your side of the sea, and we on ours.

But the feeling of abhorrence which is not, at such a moment as this, sternly and incessantly translated into deeds is of no account! So let me return to a last survey of the War. On my home journey from Nancy, I passed through Paris, and was again welcomed at G.H.Q. on my way to Boulogne. In Paris, the breathless news of the Germans' quickening retreat on the Somme and the Aisne was varied one morning by the welcome tidings of the capture of Bagdad; and at the house of one of the most distinguished of European publicists, M. Joseph Reinach, of the *Figaro*, I met, on our passage through, the lively, vigorous man, with his look of Irish vivacity and force—M. Painlevé—who only a few days later was to succeed General Lyautey as French Minister for War. At our own headquarters, I found opinion as quietly confident as before. We were on the point of entering Bapaume; the "pushing up" was going extraordinarily well, owing to the excellence of the staff-work, and the energy and efficiency of all the auxiliary services—the Engineers, and the Labour Battalions, all the makers of roads and railways, the builders of huts, and levellers of shell-broken ground. And the vital importance of the long struggle on the Somme was becoming every day more evident. Only about Russia, both in Paris and at G.H.Q., was there a kind of silence which meant great anxiety. Lord Milner and General Castelnau had returned from Petrograd. In Paris, at any rate, it was not believed that they brought good news. All the huge efforts of the Allies to supply Russia with money, munitions, and transport, were they to go for nothing, owing to some sinister and thwarting influence which seemed to be strangling the national life?

Then a few days after my return home, the great explosion came, and when the first tumult and dust of it cleared away, there, indeed, was a strangely altered Europe! From France, Great Britain, and America went up a great cry of sympathy, of congratulation. The Tsardom was gone!—the "dark forces" had been overthrown; the political exiles were free; and Freedom seemed to stand there on the Russian soil shading her bewildered eyes against the sun of victory, amazed at her own deed.

But ten weeks have passed since then, and it would be useless to disguise that the outburst of warm and sincere rejoicing that greeted the overthrow of the Russian autocracy has passed once more into anxiety. Is Russia going to count any more in this great struggle for a liberated Europe, or will the forces of revolution devour each other, till in the course of time the fated "saviour of society" appears, and old tyrannies come back? General Smuts, himself the hero of a national struggle which has ended happily for both sides and the world, has been giving admirable expression here to the thoughts of many hearts. First of all to the emotion with which all lovers of liberty have seen the all but bloodless fall of the old tyranny. "It might have taken another fifty years or a century of tragedy and suffering to have brought it about! But the enormous strain of this war has done it, and the Russian people stand free in their own house." Now, what will they do with their freedom? Ten weeks have passed, and the Russian armies are still disorganised, the Russian future uncertain. Meanwhile Germany has been able to throw against the Allies in France, and Austria has been able to throw against Italy on the Isonzo, forces which they think they need no longer against Russia, and the pace of victory has thereby been slackened. But General Smuts makes his eloquent appeal to the Russia which once held and broke Napoleon:

"Liberty is like young wine—it mounts to your head sometimes, and liberty, as a force in the world, requires organisation and discipline.... There must be organisation, and there must be discipline. The Russian people are learning to-day the greatest lesson of life—that to be free you must work very hard and struggle very hard. They have the sensation of freedom, now that their bonds and shackles are gone, and no doubt they feel the joy, the intoxication, of their new experience; but they are living in a world which is not governed by formulas, however cleverly devised, but in a world of brute force, and unless that is smashed, even liberty itself will suffer and cannot live."

Will the newly-freed forget those that are still suffering and bound?
Will Russia forget Belgium?—and forget Serbia?

"Serbia was the reason why we went to war. She was going to be crushed under the Austrian heel, and Russia said this shall not be allowed. Serbia has in that way become the occasion probably of the greatest movement for freedom the world has ever seen. Are we going to forget Serbia? No! We must stand by those martyr peoples who have stood by the great forces of the world. If the great democracies of the world become tired, if they become faint, if they halt by the way, if they leave those little ones in the lurch, then they shall pay for it in wars more horrible than human mind can foresee. I am sure we shall stand by those little ones. They have gone under, but we have not gone under. England and America, France and Russia, have not gone under, and we shall see them through, and shame on us if ever the least thought enters our minds of not seeing them through."

* * * * *

Noble and sincere words! One can but hope that the echoes of them may reach the ear and heart of Russia.

But if towards Russia the sky that seemed to have cleared so suddenly is at present clouded and obscure—"westward, look, the land is bright!"

A fortnight after the abdication of the Tsar, Congress met in Washington, and President Wilson's speech announcing war between Germany and America had rung through the world. All that you, sir, the constant friend and champion of the Allies, and still more of their cause, and all that those who feel with you in the States have hoped for so long, is now to be fulfilled. It may take some time for your country, across those thousand miles of sea, to *realise* the war, to feel it in every nerve, as we do. But in these seven weeks—how much you have done, as well as said! You have welcomed the British mission in a way to warm our British hearts; you have shown the French mission how passionately America feels for France. You have sent us American destroyers, which have already played their part in a substantial reduction of the submarine losses. You have lent the Allies 150 millions sterling. You have passed a Bill which will ultimately give you an army of two million men. You are raising such troops as will immediately increase the number of Americans in France to 100,000—equalling five German divisions. You are sending us ten thousand doctors to England and France, and hundreds of them have already arrived. You have doubled the personnel of your Navy, and increased your Regular Army by nearly 180,000 men. You are constructing 3,500 aeroplanes, and training 6,000 airmen. And you are now talking of 100,000 aeroplanes! Not bad, for seven weeks!

* * * * *

For the Allies also those seven weeks have been full of achievement. On Easter Monday, April 9th, the Battle of Arras began, with the brilliant capture by the Canadians of that very Vimy Ridge I had seen on March 2nd, from the plateau of Notre Dame de Lorette, lying in the middle distance under the spring sunshine. That exposed hill-side—those batteries through which I had walked—those crowded roads, and travelling guns, those marching troops and piled ammunition dumps!—how the recollection of them gave accent and fire to the picture of the battle as the telegrams from the front built it up day by day before one's eyes! Week by week, afterwards, with a mastery in artillery and in aviation that nothing could withstand, the British Army pushed on through April. After the first great attack which gave us the Vimy Ridge and brought our line close to Lens in the north, and to the neighbourhood of Bullecourt in the south, the 23rd of April saw the second British advance, which gave us Gravrelle and Guemappe, and made further breaches in the Hindenburg line. On April 16th the French made their magnificent attack in Champagne, with 10,000 prisoners on the first day (increased to 31,000 by May 24th)—followed by the capture of the immensely important positions of Moronvillers and Craonne. Altogether the Allies in little more than a month took 50,000 prisoners, and large numbers of guns. General Allenby, for instance, captured 150 guns, General Home 64, while General Byng formed three "Pan-Germanic groups" out of his. We recovered many square miles of the robbed territory of France—40 villages one day, 100 villages another; while the condition in which the Germans had left both the recovered territory and its inhabitants has steeled once more the determination of the nations at war with Germany to put an end to "this particular form of ill-doing on the part of an uncivilised race."

During May there has been no such striking advance on either the French or British fronts, though Roeux and Bullecourt, both very important points, from their bearing on the Drocourt-Quéant line, behind which lie Douai and Cambrai, have been captured by the British, and the French have continuously bettered their line and defied the most desperate counter-attacks. But May has been specially Italy's month! The Italian offensive on the Isonzo, and the Carso, beginning on May 14th, in ten days achieved more than any onlooker had dared to hope. In the section between Tolmino and Gorizia where the Isonzo runs in a fine gorge, the western bank belonging to Italy, and the eastern to Austria, all the important heights on the eastern bank across the river, except one that may fall to them any day, have been carried by the superb fighting of the Italians, amongst whom Dante's fellow citizens, the Florentine regiment, and regiments drawn from the rich Tuscan hills have specially distinguished themselves. While on the Carso, that rock-wilderness which stretches between Gorizia and Trieste, where fighting, especially in hot weather, supplies a supreme test of human endurance, the Italians have pushed on and on, from point to point, till now they are within ten miles of Trieste. British artillery is with the Italian Army, and British guns have been shelling military quarters and stores in the outskirts of Trieste, while British monitors are co-operating at sea. The end is not yet, for the Austrians will fight to their last man for Trieste; and owing to the Russian situation the Austrians have been able to draw reinforcements from Galicia, which have seriously stiffened the task of Italy. But the omens are all good, and the Italian nation is more solidly behind its army than ever before.

So that in spite of the apparent lull in the Allied offensive on the French front, during the later weeks of May, all has really been going well. The only result of the furious German attempts to recover the ground lost in April has been to exhaust the strength of the attackers; and the Allied cause is steadily profited thereby. Our own troops have never been more sure of final victory. Let me quote a soldier's plain and graphic letter, recently published:

"This break-away from trench war gives us a much better time. We know now that we are the top dogs, and that we are keeping the Germans on the move. And they're busy wondering all the time; they don't know where the next whack is coming from. Mind you, I'm far from saying that we can get them out of the Hindenburg line without a lot of fighting yet, but it is only a question of time. It's a different sensation going over the top now from what it was in the early days. You see, we used to know that our guns were not nearly so many as the Germans', and that we hadn't the stuff to put over. Now we just climb out of a trench and walk behind a curtain of fire. It makes a difference. It seems to me we are steadily beating the Boche at his own game. He used to be strong in the matter of guns, but that's been taken from him. He used gas—do you remember the way the Canadians got the first lot? Well, now our gas shells are a bit too strong for him, and so are our flame shells. I bet he wishes now that he hadn't thought of his flame-throwers! ... Then there's another thing, and that's the way our chaps keep improving. The Fritzes are not so good as they used to be. You get up against a bunch now and again that fight well, but we begin to see more of the 'Kamerad' business. It's as much up to the people at home to see this thing through as it is to the men out here. We need the guns and shells to blow the Germans out of the strong places that they've had years to build and dig, and the folks at home can leave the rest to us. We can do the job all right if they back us up and don't get tired. I think we've shown them that too. You'll get all that from the papers, but maybe it comes better from a soldier. You can take it from me that it's true. I've seen the beginning, and I've been in places where things were pretty desperate for us, and I've seen *the start of the finish*. The difference is marvellous. I've only had an army education, and it might strike you that I'm not able to judge. I'm a soldier though, and I look at it as a soldier. I say, give us the stuff, keep on giving us the tools and the men to use them, and—it may be soon or it may be long—we'll beat the Boche to his knees."

The truth seems to be that the Germans are outmatched, first and foremost, in aircraft and in guns. You will remember the quiet certainty of our young Flight-Commander on March 1st—"When the next big offensive comes, we shall down them, just as we did on the Somme." The prophecy has been made good, abundantly good!—at the cost of many a precious life. The air observation on our side has been far better and more daring than that on the German side; and the work of our artillery has been proportionately more accurate and more effective.

As to guns and ammunition, "the number of heavy shells fired in the first week of the present offensive"—says an official account—"was nearly twice as great as it was in the first week of the Somme offensive, and in the second week it was 6-1/2 times as great as it was in the second week of the Somme offensive. As a result of this great artillery fire, which had never been exceeded in the whole course of the war, a great saving of British life has been effected." And no praise can be too high for our gunners. In a field where, two years ago, Germany had the undisputed predominance, we have now beaten her alike in the supply of guns and in the daring and efficiency of our gunners.

Nevertheless, let there be no foolish underestimate of the still formidable strength of the Germans. The British and French missions will have brought to your Government all available information on this point. There can be no doubt that a "wonderful" effort, as one of our Ministers calls it, has been made by Germany during the past winter. She has mobilised all her people for the war as she has never done yet. She has increased her munitions and put fresh divisions in the field. The estimates of her present fighting strength given by our military writers and correspondents do not differ very much.

Colonel Repington, in *The Times*, puts the German fighting men on both fronts at 4,500,000, with 500,000 on the lines of communication, and a million in the German depots. Mr. Belloc's estimate is somewhat less, but not materially different. Both writers agree that we are in presence of Germany's last and greatest effort, that she has no more behind, and that if the Allies go on as they have begun—and now with the help of America—this summer should witness the fulfilment at least of that forecast which I reported to you in my earlier letters as so general among the chiefs of our Army in France—*i.e.* "this year will see the war *decided*, but may not see it ended." Since I came home, indeed, more optimistic prophecies have reached me from France. For some weeks after the American declaration of war, "We shall be home by Christmas!" was the common cry—and amongst some of the best-informed.

But the Russian situation has no doubt: reacted to some extent on these April hopes. And it is clear that, during April and early May, under the stimulus of the submarine successes, German spirits have temporarily revived. Never have the Junkers been more truculent, never have the Pan-Germans talked wilder nonsense about "annexation" and "indemnities." Until quite recently at any rate, the whole German nation—except no doubt a cautious and intelligent few at the real sources of information—believed that the submarine campaign would soon "bring England to her knees." They were so confident, that they ran the last great risk—they brought America into the War!

How does it look now? The situation is still critical and dangerous. But I recall the half-smiling prophecy of my naval host, in the middle of March, as we stood together on the deck of his ship, looking over his curtseying and newly-hatched flock of destroyers gathered round him in harbour. Was it not, perhaps, as near the mark as that of our airmen hosts on March 1st has proved itself to be? "Have patience and you'll see great things! The situation is serious, but quite healthy." Two months, and a little more, since the words were spoken:—and week by week, heavy as it still is, the toll of submarine loss is at least kept in check, and your Navy, now at work with ours—most fitting and welcome Nemesis!—is helping England to punish and baffle the "uncivilised race," who, if they had their way, would blacken and defile for ever the old and glorious record of man upon the sea. You, who store such things in your enviable memory, will recollect how in the Odyssey, that kindly race of singers and wrestlers, the Phaeacians, are the escorts and conveyers of all who need and ask for protection at sea. They keep the waterways for civilised men, against pirates and assassins, as your nation and ours mean to keep them in the future. It is true that a treacherous sea-god, jealous of any interference with his right to slay and drown at will, smote the gallant ship that bore Odysseus safely home, on her return, and made a rock of her for ever. Poseidon may stand for the Kaiser of the story. He is gone, however, with all his kin! But the humane and civilising tradition of the sea, which this legend carries back into the dawn of time—it shall be for the Allies—shall it not?—in this war, to rescue it, once and for ever, from the criminal violence which would stain the free paths of ocean with the murder and sudden death of those who have been in all history the objects of men's compassion and care—the wounded, the helpless, the woman, and the child.

* * * * *

For the rest, let me gather up a few last threads of this second instalment of our British story.

Of that vast section of the war concerned with the care and transport of the wounded, and the health of the Army, it is not my purpose to speak at length in these Letters. Like everything else it has been steadily and eagerly perfected during the past year. Never have the wounded in battle, in any war, been so tenderly and skilfully cared for;—never have such intelligence and goodwill been applied to the health conditions of such huge masses of men. Nor is it necessary to dwell again, as I did last year, on the wonderful work of women in the war. It has grown in complexity and bulk; women-workers in munitions are now nearly a fifth of the whole body; but essentially the general aspect of it has not changed much in the last twelve months.

But what has changed is *the food situation*, owing partly to submarine attack, and partly to the general shortage in the food-supply of the world. In one of my earlier letters I spoke with anxiety of the still unsettled question—Will the house-wives and mothers of the nation realise—in time—our food necessities? Will their thrift-work in the homes complete the munition-work of women in the factories? Or must we submit to the ration-system, with all its cumbrous inequalities, and its hosts of officials; because the will and intelligence of our people, which have risen so remarkably to the other tasks of this war, are not equal to the task of checking food consumption without compulsion?

It looks now as though they would be equal. Since my earlier letter the country has been more and more generally covered with the National War Savings Committees which have been carrying into food-economy the energy they spent originally on the raising of the last great War Loan. The consumption of bread and flour throughout the country has gone down—not yet sufficiently—but enough to show that the idea has taken hold:—"*Save bread, and help victory!*" And since your declaration of war it strengthens our own effort to know that America with her boundless food-supplies is standing by, and that her man-and sea-power are now to be combined with ours in defeating the last effort of Germany to secure by submarine piracy what she cannot win on the battle-field.

Meanwhile changes which will have far-reaching consequences after the war are taking place in our own home food-supply. The long neglect of our home agriculture, the slow and painful dwindling of our country populations, are to come to an end. The Government calls for the sowing of three million additional acres of wheat in Great Britain; and throughout the country the steam tractors are at work ploughing up land which has either never borne wheat, or which has ceased to bear it for nearly a century. Thirty-five thousand acres of corn land are to be added to the national store in this county of Hertfordshire alone. The wages of agricultural labourers, have risen by more than one-third. The farmers are to be protected and encouraged as they never have been since the Cobdenite revolution; and the Corn Production Bill now passing through Parliament shows what the grim lesson of this war has done to change the old and easy optimism of our people.

As to the energy that has been thrown into other means of food-supply, let the potatoes now growing in the flower-beds in front of Buckingham Palace stand for a symbol of it! The potato-crop of this year—barring accidents—will be enormous; and the whole life of our country villages has been quickened by the effort that has been made to increase the produce of the cottage gardens and allotments. The pride and pleasure of the women and the old men in what they have been able to do at home, while their sons and husbands are fighting at the front, is moving to see. Food prices are very high; life in spite of increased wages is hard. But the heart of England is set on winning this war; and the letters which pass between the fathers and mothers in this village where I live, and the sons at the front, in whom they take a daily and hourly pride, would not give Germany much comfort could she read them. I take this little scene, as an illustration, fresh from the life of my own village:

Imagine a visitor, on behalf of the food-economy movement, endeavouring to persuade a village mother to come to some cookery lessons organised by the local committee.

Mrs. S. is discovered sitting at a table on which are preparations for a meal. She receives the visitor and the visitor's remarks with an air—quite unconscious—of tragic meditation; and her honest labour-stained hand sweeps over the things on the table.

"Cheese!"—she says, at last—"*eightpence* the 'arf pound!"

A pause. The hand points in another direction.

"*Lard—sevenpence*—that scrubby little piece! *Sugar*! sixpence 'a'penny the pound. The best part of two shillin's gone! Whatever *are* we comin' to?"

Gloom descends on the little kitchen. The visitor is at a loss—when suddenly the round, motherly face changes.—"But *there* now! I'm goin' to smile, whatever 'appens. I'm not one as is goin' to give in! And we 'ad a letter from Arthur [her son in the trenches] this morning, to say 'is Company's on the list for leave, and 'e's applied.—Oh dear, Miss, just to *think* of it!"

Then, with a catch in her voice:

"But it's not the comin' home, Miss—it's *the goin' back again*! Yes, I'll come to the cookin', Miss, if I *possibly* can!"

There's the spirit of our country folk—patriotic, patient, true.

As to labour conditions generally. I spoke, perhaps, in my first letter rather too confidently, for the moment, of the labour situation. There has been one serious strike among the engineers since I began to write, and a good many minor troubles. But neither the Tyne nor the Clyde was involved, and though valuable time was lost, in the end the men were brought back to work quite as much by the pressure of public opinion among their own comrades, men and women, as by any Government action. The Government have since taken an important step from which much is hoped, by dividing up the country into districts and appointing local commissioners to watch over and, if they can, remove the causes of "unrest"—causes which are often connected with the inevitable friction of a colossal transformation, and sometimes with the sheer fatigue of the workers, whose achievement—munition-workers, ship-wrights, engineers— during these three years has been nothing short of marvellous.

As to finance, the colossal figures of last year, of which I gave a summary in *England's Effort,* have been much surpassed. The Budget of Great Britain for this year, including advances to our Allies, reaches the astounding figure of two thousand three hundred million sterling. Our war expenditure is now close upon six million sterling a day (£5,600,000). Of this the expenditure on the Army and Navy and munitions has risen from a daily average of nearly three millions sterling, as it stood last year, to a daily average of nearly five millions.

But the nation has not spent in vain!

"Compare the first twenty-four days of the fighting on the Somme last year,"—said Mr. Bonar Law in a recent speech—"with the first twenty-four days of the operations of this spring. Four times as much territory had been taken from the enemy in this offensive as was taken in the Somme, against the resistance of double the number of German divisions. And of those divisions just one-half have had to be withdrawn—shattered—from the fighting line while the British casualties in the offensive have been from 50 to 75 per cent, less than the casualties in the Somme fighting."

Consider, too, the news which is still fresh as I finish this letter—(June 11th)—of the victory of Messines; perhaps the most complete, the most rounded success—so far—that has fallen to the British armies in the war! Last year, in three months' fighting on the Somme, we took the strongly fortified Albert ridge, and forced the German retreat of last February. On April 8th of this year began the battle of Arras which gave us the Vimy Ridge, and a free outlook over the Douai plain. And finally, on June 7th, four days ago, the Messines ridge, which I saw last year on March 2nd—apparently impregnable and inaccessible!—from a neighbouring hill, with the German trenches scored along its slopes, was captured by General Plumer and his splendid army in a few hours, after more than twelve months' preparation, with lighter casualties than have ever fallen to a British attack before, with heavy losses to the enemy, large captures of guns, and 7,000 prisoners. Our troops have since moved steadily forward; and the strategic future is rich in possibilities. The Germans have regained nothing; and the German press has not yet dared to tell the German people of the defeat. Let us remember also the victorious campaign of this year in Mesopotamia; and the welcome stroke of the past week in Greece, by which King "Tino" has been at last dismissed, and the Liberal forces of the Greek nation set free.

* * * * *

Aye, we do consider—we do remember—these things! We feel that the goal is drawing slowly but steadily nearer, that ultimate victory is certain, and with victory, the dawn of a better day for Europe. But who, least of all a woman, can part from the tragic spectacle of this war without bitterness of spirit?

"Who will give us back our children?"

Wickedness and wrong will find their punishment, and the dark Hours now passing, in the torch-race of time, will hand the light on to Hours of healing and of peace. But the dead return not. It is they whose appealing voices seem to be in the air to-day, as we think of America.

Among the Celts of ancient Brittany there was a belief which still survives in the traditions of the Breton peasants and in the name of part of the Breton coast. Every All Souls' Night, says a story at least as old as the sixth century, the souls of the dead gather on the cliffs of Brittany, above that bay which is still called the "Bai des Trépassés," waiting for their departure across the ocean to a far region of the west, where the gods sit for judgment, and the good find peace. On that night, the fishermen hear at midnight mysterious knockings at their doors. They go down to the water's edge, and behold, there are boats unknown to them, with no visible passengers. But the fishermen take the oars, and though they see nothing, they feel the presence of the souls crowding into the boats, and they row, on and on, into the west, past the farthest point of any land they know. Suddenly, they feel the boats lightened of all that weight of spirits, and the souls are gone—streaming out with solemn cries and longing into the wide illimitable ocean of the west, in search of some invisible shore.

So now the call of those hundreds of thousands who have given their young lives—so beloved, so rich in promise!—for their country and the freedom of men, is in your ears and ours. The dead are witnesses of the compact between you and us. For that cause to which they brought their ungrudged sacrifice has now laid its resistless claim on you. Together, the free peoples of Europe and America have now to carry it to victory —victory, just, necessary, and final.

MARY A. WARD.